Praise for *Count Me In*

"Fun and flirty, *Count Me In* is a perfect companion to your summer vacation."
- Sarah Monzon, author of *All of You*

"Mikal Dawn's debut novel is such a fun combination of tenderness, romance, and tickle-your-funnybone humor. Combine an adventure-loving hero and his sordid past with an accident-prone, feet-on-the-ground heroine and her mountain of worries, and you have a delightful romance that shows how love gives us the courage to soar beyond our insecurities. Allegra is such a likeable and relatable heroine, second-guessing herself, but working hard to help others achieve their dreams. Ty is a kind-hearted hero who's learned the value of what matters most. Don't miss out on this delightful debut!"
- Pepper Basham, author of *Just the Way You Are* and the Penned in Time series.

Praise for *If She Dares*

"I can't say enough about how this book gives me the giggles and warms my heart... Mikal Dawn...brings humor, and sparks of adventure to her books."
- Marylin Furumasu, MF Literary Works

# Claim My Heart

## Mikal Dawn

121 PUBLISHING HOUSE
*I lift my eyes to the mountains...*

Cover photos:
Front cover design by: Mikal Hermanns
Back cover design by: Teresa Tysinger, https://teresatysinger.com/
Seattle Christmas Skyline: mauromod/depositphotos.com
Wooden gavel, glasses and books: mitay20/depositphotos.com
Portrait of a Chinese family: Roomyana/depositphotos.com

First edition, 121 Publishing House, 2019

ISBN-13: 978-1-7337830-1-9

For Jesus. Always first. This is all because of You.

For Anike, thank you for being such a huge fan and an even bigger sweetheart. I hope one day I get to read your own stories!

# *C*hapter

# *O*ne

*H*uang Li Na peered out the window that exchanged Denver snow with Seattle drizzle and eyed the worker bees on the ground, driving around their carts, pushing planes, and waving those glow stick things like they were doing the Macarena. There was no going back now.

"Welcome to Seattle, where it's a depressing thirty-three degrees Fahrenheit and no snow to show for it. As our Captain James puts pedal to the metal to get you to our gate in record-time, please remember to check the overhead bins for your belongings. If you forget anything, please make sure it's something of value that we'll be happy to take home or sell for a tidy profit. As always, thank you for flying Northwest Airlines, where we're happy to take you for a ride."

Laughter rang throughout the plane, but Li wasn't having it. She couldn't believe she was actually doing this. And she could only imagine what her father was thinking right now. She glanced at the silver watch on her left wrist. Yep, he was likely awake and beside himself.

*She* was beside herself. While she was prepared for this by taking the uniform bar exam as her father had, enabling her to practice law in both Colorado and Washington, impersonating another lawyer could ruin any chance of a career she might have imagined.

Psh. Could? It would, if she was found out. And as her mother always said, "Concealing the truth is like wearing embroidered clothes and traveling by night."

Yeah. She had no idea what that meant, but she loved remembering her mother's voice. Let's just hope she wouldn't also have to work to remember her father's voice just yet.

Cancer. She shuddered as she unbuckled the seat belt and stood.

Her chest rose as she swallowed a deep breath. No sense in dwelling on what might happen when she had a big job ahead of her.

Her heart thudded against her chest. She still couldn't believe she took her father's plane ticket. Thank goodness they kind of shared a name. She'd half expected the police to storm the jet and remove her by force after she boarded in Denver, but they never came. Now that she was finally at the gate in Seattle, however, those nerves came pounding back. What if the police caught on? Or worse...what if her father came after her? Jail she could handle, but her father's disappointment? *Lord, have mercy.* She might be able to pull off an orange jumpsuit—actually, no. Maybe not. It would likely wash her out and make her look ill. Hm.

Wait, what was she doing? Oh sheesh. She would rather go to prison than face her father, apparently. But it'd be free room and board. And maybe she'd get out of her student loans? Ooohhh...

"Miss?"

Li Na jumped, for the first time thankful she was so short—she missed hitting her skull on the overhead bin. She turned to find a flight attendant watching her.

"Are you okay, miss? I'm sorry I scared you."

"No, I mean yes. I'm fine. It's okay. I was lost in my own little world." She flicked her gaze up and over the attendant's shoulder. No police. Maybe she could pull this off after all. She pasted on a smile. "I'm fine, thank you. Just daydreaming. You know how it is. Just wondering if the cops are about to storm the flight. Or is it TSA? Or sheriffs?" Li tilted her head and tapped her bottom lip. "Or do they have special police for planes? No wait! It's the U.S. Marshals, isn't it?" She gazed at the flight attendant.

Oops. Way to stay inconspicuous.

The woman—Chrissy, according to her nametag—took a small step back, a smile baring her teeth. Or a grimace.

Definitely a grimace.

She'd better stop while she was ahead, or Chrissy would call whomever it was that stormed the doors of planes and forced people off in order to arrest them. She didn't want to be one of those people that ended up on YouTube.

Chrissy placed a gentle hand on Li's shoulder. "Miss, everyone has disembarked. Do you need any assistance?"

Her heart raced faster than Marco Andretti on the Indianapolis Motor Speedway. Time to make her escape.

"I'm good, honest."

Li grabbed her carry on from the overhead bin—the only piece of luggage she had in order to keep things as simple and fast at the airport as possible, scooched past the attendant with a quick, "Thanks," and left the confines of the plane.

As she exited the doors and looked for a Lyft or Uber, she ran over her mental checklist.

One: Find Father's ticket and literally jet. Check.

Two: Don't be nabbed by the police. She crawled into the back seat of a maroon car. "Pioneer Square," she rattled off the name of the hotel she'd be staying at for the foreseeable future. As the driver shot away from the curb, Li Na turned to look back. No police with their weapons out running after the car. Check. She faced forward and settled into her seat.

Now for step three: make the lawyer her father had been emailing the past couple of days believe she was his contact.

She dropped her head back on the seat and blew hard.

What had she done?

Colin Wen truly hoped there were no hidden cameras in or around his cubicle. If so, he imagined Darren Schultz, the senior partner "mentoring" him, would be stomping his way back down and firing him on the spot for the look Colin had just given Darren after their little chat.

Corporate law wasn't at all what he'd imagined it to be. Was it really worth leaving Ohio, his parents, and their matchmaking ways?

He pictured the stubborn set to their jaws as they matter-of-factly told him who he was going to marry. Their best friend's daughter. The same one who'd repeatedly narced on him growing up. Just because he'd been the mastermind for all the shenanigans they'd pulled as kids didn't mean she hadn't shared in the blame.

"Colin."

Glad to have his thoughts interrupted, Colin glanced up at the voice. One of the firm's paralegals, Genifer, grinned at him. "Have a nice chat with Darren?"

He was thankful he wasn't the only junior partner who squirmed whenever Darren was nearby. He was unscrupulous at best. "So nice."

She laughed. "That's what I thought. He passed by my desk and told me you needed help with the Futures IT case."

Good old Darren. Never one to trust any attorney but himself, he had eyes and ears everywhere. Or so he thought.

"Gen, am I ever glad you're on my side."

A cheeky grin surfaced. "I have way too much fun coming up with stories to tell Darren. He must know by now I'm always yanking his leg...but then, maybe not. He keeps coming to me to help everyone." She rolled her eyes. "Like any of you need serious help."

"Actually, I do." Colin shuffled some papers around and pulled a manila file out and handed it over. "A lawyer representing Futures IT is coming in from Denver in," he checked the smartwatch circling his wrist, "an hour. I wrote down some questions about the takeover on the papers in there. Could you find the answers before the meeting?"

She lifted her chin...and an eyebrow.

Right. Manners. "Please."

Genifer clicked her stilettos together—he couldn't understand how women didn't break their necks when wearing those—and snapped a cheeky salute. "You've got it." He watched for a moment as she turned and walked off. There was a time he thought he might ask her out.

You know, until he'd overheard she had a boyfriend. And since they were now married, he was relieved he hadn't asked. How awkward would that have been?

He ignored the fact if he'd stayed in Ohio, he'd likely be married by now. No way, no how. Never mind that arranged marriages often have better success rates than when people choose their own spouses. He banked on the fact that he prayed, hard, for his future wife and for God to show him who she was.

He shook his head. He'd better get his mind back on this hostile takeover. Darren had made it clear winning this case would make or break his career with Shiloh and Schultz. Little did the Hun know...

# Chapter
## Two

The towering building almost unnerved her. Okay, it did unnerve her, but she couldn't turn back.

Her handbag-pseudo briefcase vibrated. Her phone. Again. She refused to look at it, knowing it was probably her father. She couldn't talk to him yet. No doubt he would want to spend days telling her how she'd shamed him by running off with his ticket to take his place on this case. But she couldn't let him delay chemo to take this on, and his childhood friend couldn't wait. The hostile takeover was looming, and the friend was counting on her father to get him out of it.

And she had no clue what she was doing.

Squealing bus tires jolted her out of her thoughts. There was no time like the present. Inhaling until her lungs burned, she stepped through the doors and into a lobby with white marble floors and floor-to-ceiling glass windows. A bank of elevators lined up like teeth behind a security desk opened and closed, moving people up and down at their will. Li stood behind two men showing their identification to the security guard. When they walked through the metal detector, she stepped up to the guard.

"I.D., please."

This was it. Truly it. Li wordlessly passed her driver's license to the guard. His ebony skin glowed under the sunlight streaming in through the windows, making it look flawless.

She was kind of jealous. She'd flown into Seattle with a pimple developing near her nose. No doubt from stress. Or deceit. Could deceit cause pimples? Probably.

Li watched as the man entered her name into a computer. "You're a little early, but that's good. Those lawyers can't stand people who are late." He grinned and handed her license back to her. "Good luck up there. You'll need it."

She didn't know words could cause her stomach to roil. But again, that was probably just the deceit doing its nasty work. "I will?"

"Oh yeah," he sat up straight. "Especially if you're meeting with one of the upper ranks. Let me tell you, they're downright nightmares."

Wonderful. "How so?"

She regretted asking. Oh, how she regretted it.

"One of them took a young man to task—one of the only lawyers I like, mind you—right here in the lobby. Threatened him an' all. Said if he didn't follow through, he'd see him blacklisted."

Hoping to stop him, she cleared her throat. No such luck.

"Then he hauled off and threw his briefcase on the floor, slammed a foot down, and his face...I never seen a face that red before. And the volume." He slapped his knee. "My ears rang for days afterward."

She stared at the man, wrinkles surrounding teeth yellowed by coffee, if the stained mug on the desk in front of him was any clue. His bushy white brows lifted.

"You okay, miss? You want me to call you another cab so you can get outta here while you're still alive?"

The thought of bright orange jumpsuits and cellmates named "Crazy Eyes" ran through her mind. Maybe prison wouldn't be so bad. Did Mr. Fu *really* need to maintain control of his company?

Elevators chimed and whooshed around her. Her stomach lurched, but she murmured a "Thanks" to the guard, walked through the metal detector to the sound of the guard cackling, grabbed her things, and stepped up to one of the elevators just as the door slid open and a group of suits walked out. In she went, pressing button 14. Thank goodness they weren't glass elevators, looking out over the city. Fourteen floors wasn't so high in a skyline like Seattle, but it was high enough to make her sweat if she had to see the vantage point.

All too soon, the doors opened up to Shiloh and Schultz. Huh. She'd expected a way posher setting. Instead, she was greeted by the same marble floors as the lobby, but with a much more clinical set-up. Straight ahead was the receptionist's desk with the firm's sign lettered in gold hanging behind and just above her head. Li wondered if they'd made her sit there while they hung it to make sure she didn't block any of it. To the right was a bank of burgundy chairs, a glass and gold coffee table with magazines scattered over it, and a common abstract print hanging on the wall. To the left, glass doors led to what looked like offices and cubicles. Li stepped forward to the desk in front of her.

A woman with salt and pepper hair up in a neat bun looked up and smiled. "Good morning. Do you have an appointment?"

Li looked at the nameplate on the woman's desk. Pamela Harrison.

She swallowed. Here goes nothing. "Yes. Huang Li for Colin Wen." She left the "Na" out of her name. It was the only part of her name she didn't share with her father.

"Why don't you go have a seat, and I'll let Mr. Wen know you've arrived."

"Thank you." Li moved toward the burgundy chairs, eyeing the magazines. The Wall Street Journal and The American Lawyer joined Lawyer Monthly and New Law Journal. In other words, nothing interesting. At least not to her.

Her stomach a jumble, she pulled out her notes to focus on those instead. Not that there was any use in doing so; Pamela stood.

"Ms. Li? Please follow me. I'll show you to the boardroom."

Ms. Li. She was used to people getting it wrong by now. She was raised by second-generation Chinese-Americans, but her family still kept the Chinese ways of naming people, with the surname first and the first name second. It confused a lot of people, including this receptionist, but they were honest mistakes. Hopefully Li wouldn't be here for more than just today, so she didn't correct Pamela.

The woman led her through the glass doors and past the bank of offices to a room with one large, dark wood table, twelve chairs that mirrored the ones in the lobby, and a waist-high buffet that matched the table. On the buffet sat a Keurig and a mini refrigerator. The windows overlooked the busy street fourteen floors below. No way was she going to get near those things. The last thing she wanted to do was embarrass herself by getting sick all over her opponent's windows.

Afraid of heights? Yup. And she had no shame in it.

"Can I get you anything to drink?"

Li placed her briefcase on a chair with her back to the windows. No sense in sitting where she could see and remember just how high she was. "Please. Water?"

Pamela reached to open the mini fridge and plucked out a bottle. She brought it, along with a coaster embedded with the firm's logo, over and placed it in front of Li. "Would you like anything to eat?"

She looked down at her watch. Eleven o'clock. Not lunchtime, but too close to it that if she ate a snack, she wouldn't be hungry. And she hoped beyond hope to be out of here with the legal matter settled before noon. A pie in the sky dream. "No, thank you."

The older woman nodded, smiled, and said, "Mr. Wen will be right in."

"Thank you."

Pamela closed the door behind her. Left on her own, Li pulled the papers she'd gathered from her father's desk back in Denver out of her briefcase, along with a black and a red pen, and organized everything in front of her.

From what she'd read while waiting to board the plane—she'd needed something to distract her from thoughts of being hauled off by police—her father's friend owned an IT company who was in the middle of a hostile takeover. And so far, it was a losing battle.

Footsteps sounded outside the room. Li grabbed the bottle of water and took a long drink. Her mouth was so dry. From the travel? Or nerves? She scoffed. Probably nerves. She was sure she'd have an ulcer by the end of this.

The door opened and in walked...Adonis? It had to be Adonis.

God must have taken great pride in this creation of beauty. Oh, where was her water?

Li looked at her hand. Where the bottle of water was being squeezed to the end of its life. Enough so that water was dangerously close to pouring out the opening.

<hr />

"Thanks, Pam." Colin grabbed the folder from his desk then did a quick check in the reflection of his computer monitor to make sure his tie was straight. He stood and made his way toward the boardroom, reading the last email he'd received from Huang Li. He sounded like a good guy who really just wanted his client to keep his business going in his own way.

"Colin," Genifer's voice stopped him in his tracks. She caught up, handing him a sheaf of papers. "Here are the opinions I found for your questions. Sorry it took a little longer." She glanced over her shoulder then took a step closer to him and whispered, "What are you doing? Those questions you needed answers to...Colin, if you're thinking what I think you're thinking..." She let her words trail off.

He smiled his thanks. "Much appreciated."

"Colin."

Gen's eyes widened and Colin bit back a groan. How he hoped the Hun hadn't heard Genifer's whisper. He turned to face Darren, who had no clue of the nickname christened upon him by the junior staff. Or if he did have a clue, he was proud of it. Colin wouldn't put it past him.

"Yes, Mr. Schultz."

Darren peered past Colin's shoulder and jutted his chin, waving Genifer away. Colin didn't dare take his eyes off the senior partner; he demanded one hundred percent attention at all times when he was around.

Hun met his gaze. "I want this deal done before Christmas. Remember, your position here at Shiloh and Schultz depends on it."

Never mind that hostile takeovers could take months. And never mind that they often resulted in failure. Hun didn't care about that, nor did he care about Colin and his position here. Darren was always reminding everyone that there were lawyers graduating from law school every year who would jump at the chance to get into an established firm right off the bat.

"Yes, Mr. Schultz."

Hun turned back into his office and shut the door behind him. A deep breath to calm the bees stinging his stomach, and Colin stepped toward the boardroom, refusing to look through the windows to get a glimpse of the lawyer he'd be dealing with. Reaching the closed door, he paused, took two more breaths, and turned the knob.

Inside, he opened his mouth to welcome Huang Li, but the sight in front of him robbed him of words.

Huang Li wasn't a man.

Not at all.

The woman staring at him like she'd just seen the largest slice of chocolate cake ever served on earth had smooth hair that, with the sunlight streaming in from the bank of windows behind her, proved to be true black.

She was stunning.

Yeah, definitely not the middle-aged man he'd expected.

Annnnd...he was staring at her like *he'd* just seen the largest slice of chocolate cake ever served on earth.

He loved chocolate cake.

# Chapter

# Three

If she died in this moment, it would be from asphyxiation. Because the Adonis in front of her was taking her breath away.

But at least she'd die happy.

"Huang Li?"

Her death might be a little less happy. His voice came out in a croak. Maybe he was just sick?

"Y-yes." Huh. Her own voice sounded like a frog, too. Did she catch something on the plane? Oh, she hoped not. She wanted to be back in her own bed, taking care of her father by tomorrow. Could she manage it? She had to. There was no way she wanted Father to be alone any longer than necessary.

The man strode to a seat across the table from her, set his folder down, then leaned over and held his hand out to her. Li stood, brushed her hand down the front of her skirt—she didn't want to take the chance it was damp from nerves—accepted his shake, and placed her behind back in the seat underneath her.

He cleared his throat and said, "I, uh, I'm Colin Wen." He pushed the hand she just shook through his slight pompadour as he sat.

Oooo...his voice isn't croaky. More like melted butter—smooth and warm.

He chuckled. "I'm embarrassed to admit this, but I had the impression that you were an older man."

Warmth crept across her chest. Had her father said something in his emails to Mr. Wen? Her mind flipped through the correspondence she'd read on the trip to Seattle. She didn't remember anything, but maybe she'd missed an email?

She hissed between her teeth. Maybe Father had called him? Oh no! *Think, Li, think!* She pasted on a smile and hoped beyond hope they hadn't talked on the phone. "I get that often when people read my emails before meeting me. I'm told I sound like an old man when I write." *Forgive me, Father. I promise you aren't old!*

Mr. Wen grinned. "Well, that makes me feel a bit better." The slashes of brows above his walnut-colored eyes furrowed. "Though I could have sworn Hun called you 'mister.'"

Li's eyes flicked to Mr. Wen's hands. No ring. Hun? Obviously not married, but he must be in a relationship. Though why would his girlfriend speak to Father? She had to feel him out a little more or she would never pull this charade off. "Hun?"

"What?" He slid a finger under the collar of his crisp white dress shirt. "Did I say 'Hun'? I, uh...I meant Mr. Schultz." He squeezed his eyes shut before he landed a pleading gaze on her. "He's a senior partner and, well...he, uh...the underling lawyers here, we..."

She couldn't help herself. A sputter escaped before a full-throated laugh that finally cleared her croaky voice. "So, let me guess. Hun isn't exactly a term of endearment...more like Attila?"

His well-defined bow-shaped lips tilted up. "You didn't hear it from me."

Li Na made a zipping motion across her mouth. "My lips are sealed."

The seconds ticked away on the clock as they grinned at one another. "Please call me Colin. It'll make our transaction a little more comfortable."

Ah, so he was up to an old tactic—get the opponent to loosen up and maybe they'll slip up. Not her. No way. "Please, call me Li." Two could play at this game.

"Done." He opened the file in front of him and pulled out two booklets, passing one to her. On the front was the small Futures IT logo underneath a much larger logo of the international software company that was trying to acquire Futures. Of course. A little psychology, letting her know who Goliath was...and who was David. Did Colin not know who won that little face-off?

"If you turn to page three, you'll see the financial statement of the past three years of Futures, compared to the financial statement of the acquiring company for the same period."

"Seriously? You're comparing an international company's finances to a regional company's?" Li arched one eyebrow.

Colin looked up. "This is just to show you the resources my client has in order to take over Futures." Li watched as his face turned an off-green. That was interesting. "It's really no contest."

"If you're confident in your client's abilities to pull this hostile takeover off, why invite my fa...me here?"

He watched her for a moment. "Because."

...Really? 'Because.' That's his answer?

"Because as Futures IT's attorney, I thought it only fair to find out in person what you're up against."

Step three: make the lawyer her father had been emailing the past couple of days believe she was his contact. Check. At least for now.

❧❦❧

"So, this was benevolence on your part. Not tactic?"

Colin slid his gaze to the side then down to the folder. He paused. *What do I do, Lord?* He hated knowing what this decision could mean for him, either way. He hated even more what would happen if he didn't go through with the plan he'd come up with at four o'clock this morning.

Sweat broke out on his upper lip. He stood and removed the dark grey, two-button suit jacket, revealing the four-button, double-breasted vest. Procrastinating just another minute, he unbuttoned the cuffs of his shirt and rolled them up. He didn't care if Li saw the Galatians 6:9 tattoo on his right forearm. He got it just a couple of months ago to remind him of why he entered law...and more importantly, to remind him to make the right decisions. He glanced down at the verse written on a banner over spears, the weapon the builders used in Nehemiah to guard the other builders working on the wall: Let us not grow weary in doing good.

*Let me not, Lord.* Colin met Li's gaze. "It was tactic."

Even a frown couldn't take from her beauty.

He looked over his shoulder to make sure the boardroom's door was firmly closed. It was. He turned back to Li. "I was assigned to this case against my wishes."

"Oookay." Her head tilted toward her shoulder, obviously confused.

"I went to law school with grand schemes of making a real, positive difference in Columbus. The closer I got to graduation, though, the more I chickened out." He couldn't believe he'd just admitted to a complete stranger what he couldn't even admit to himself. "So, I went down the corporate law path, thinking there was no way I could do any harm to anyone."

And yet here he was.

"I'm not sure I understand what you're saying." She picked up the water bottle in front of her and wiped a finger across the condensation that had built up on the coaster.

"I'm saying I was wrong. I've been in this firm since I graduated from law school, and it feels like all I've done is hurt the little guy in order to make the big guy more and more money. I'm constantly working on increasing my billable hours." He swallowed. "And I'm going against my conscience—against God's Word," he muttered, "in forcing a man, through his shareholders—comprised mostly of friends and family who likely don't understand what we're doing—to give up the company he's worked so hard for. All for an international giant to get their hands on some proprietary software."

Li stood and walked around the table. He was taller than average for a Chinese-American, standing at just a hair under six feet. With Li in front of him, he felt like a giant. She had to be no taller than his shoulder. He glanced down. In heels.

Her arms crossed over her chest, she stared up at him. "So...what you're telling me is—"

"What I'm telling you is that I'm probably going to be running back to Ohio with my tail tucked between my legs, but I can't do this anymore. I want to help you with this case."

If she could see her face in a mirror right now, she'd likely be embarrassed. Her mouth gaped and her eyes were the size of saucers. And yeah. She was still a vision.

"Me? You're going to help me? Isn't that unethical since you work for Goliath?"

Goliath? Ah. She saw the two IT companies as David and Goliath. Well, if he worked for Goliath right now, he knew who the winning side would be, and he wanted in. It was a big step—nope, a huge leap—of faith to leave Shiloh and Schultz, but the peace that surpassed all understanding told him it was the right leap.

"If you'll have me, I'm leaving Goliath."

Her throat bobbed. "We—I'm working pro bono."

It wasn't a shock, and he didn't expect to be paid if he joined her in this fight, but in a weird way, he was proud of her for taking this battle on for free.

Colin lifted his hand between them. "Then we're a team?"

# Chapter Four

*B*eing escorted out of the firm by building security wasn't on his to-do list, but he could write it in later...and cross it off.

And it felt good. Right. Slightly terrifying, but right.

At least they'd waited for him to shove his belongings in a box while the Hun glared at him from over the top of his cubicle, Gen standing behind him.

"You'll regret this, Wen."

"No, can't say that I will." Well, maybe a little when his savings ran out.

"You will when you can't find work in Seattle again. Trust me, I'll get you blacklisted so fast, you won't have time to sneeze."

Colin thought about that as he stood outside the building's doors, shivering from the damp cold. Blacklisted. What a terrible word, so cruel and callous. And faster than he could sneeze? He doubted that.

But...just in case, he should call his friend, Mush. Setting the box holding his belongings on the edge of a trash can on the sidewalk, Colin reached into his pocket and withdrew his cell. He swiped, looked up Mush's name, and tapped "Call."

"Munro Shackham."

"Mush, it's Wen."

"Dude, I do have call display."

Colin pulled the cell away from his ear and looked at Mush's photo, as if he could see Colin's disgust through the phone. "Then why did you answer with your name?"

"Habit. What's up?"

Colin rubbed against a tickle in his nose. "Just wanted to say hi." He rubbed again.

"In the middle of the work day?" A muffled noise over the line. Colin squeezed his eyes closed but there was no avoiding it. He sneezed. "Oh man. I just heard. What did you do?"

A knot formed in his stomach. "What do you mean?"

"You were fired?"

*What?!* Attila the Hun wasn't kidding. Literally before he could sneeze. "I wasn't fired. I quit."

"If you quit, then Schultz is going after you in a dirty way. He must have blasted an email out about you, because from what I just heard, you were caught giving confidential client information to an opposing lawyer."

Despite the cold, wet air, Colin felt sweat form on his upper lip. No. Schultz might be a dirty player, but he wouldn't be an outright liar. Would he? Colin turned his head and looked up to the fourteenth floor. Not like he could see anyone from down here, but maybe they could see him. Maybe Darren Schultz was looking down at him right now. Maybe he would see the utter contempt on Colin's face.

Yeah, he'd definitely made the right decision. No regrets.

❦

Li flopped backwards onto the hotel bed and stared up at the smooth white ceiling. If only she didn't have to call her father back. But if she didn't, she was afraid he might come after her, worried for her safety, despite the note she'd left.

And she could reassure him that not only was she working on behalf of Futures IT, but so was Colin Wen, former attorney at Shiloh and Schultz.

He would be stunned. And hopefully happy.

She slid her eyes closed. *Lord, we could use some help here.* She'd only just graduated from law school and had been working with her father in his private practice. There was no way she was versed enough in corporate law to really do justice for Mr. Fu.

"I have to do something," she whispered.

But first, the dreaded phone call. Rolling over, she reached to the chocolate-brown bedside table and unplugged her phone from the charger. Her stomach churned like a tornado. She tapped her father's name, put the phone on speaker, and laid it in front of her on the mattress.

"Léi lei." Li Na's chest warmed at the endearment. Thunder. Father said it was because she was bold, strong, and fearsome. She covered her mouth to stifle the giggle.

"You have brought me dishonor."

That giggle was appropriately stifled. "Father? I did it to save you."

"Save me?" His voice raised. "I do not need my daughter to save me!"

She blinked back tears. "If I had let you come out here, it could have taken weeks. You couldn't afford to put off your chemotherapy that long."

"That was my decision to make. I would rather die doing what is right."

Li pushed a breath past her lips. "I'm sorry. But I would rather have my father live for many years to come."

Father sighed. "They do know you are my daughter?"

Oh boy. She swallowed. "N-no. They...they believe I'm you."

"Li Na!"

"I know," she groaned. "But I didn't think you'd want anyone to know you're sick." Pride was an ugly beast, and her father had a boatload of it. "Are you going to tell them?"

Silence. Wow. *Now I know what a pregnant pause sounds like.*

"If I tell them, you may be disbarred. *I* cannot bring that dishonor upon our family."

Ooph. Talk about a guilt trip. She knew he didn't mean it as such, and maybe she deserved it, but her intentions were good.

And the road to hell is paved with good intentions. As much as she hated clichés, they had a foundation in truth, that's for sure.

Time to swallow her own pride. "Thank you, Father. I truly am sorry. I only wanted to do what I could to help you become healthy again."

"Yes, léi lei, I know." He sighed. "What are your plans?"

Li licked her lips. "I met with the opposing attorney today, Colin Wen at Shiloh and Schultz. But Father," she said, "when we met, he told me your emails convinced him he couldn't do this. He left his job there and is going to help us."

"What?"

She grinned at the lift in his voice. "Yes. And he understands it will be pro bono."

"And he is content with this?"

The peace that flashed across his face when he leaned over the table and whispered that he would help made her grin even more. His deep-set eyes sparkled with...it must have been joy.

"Yes, I think so."

"Then work hard, léi lei. My friend must keep his business."

"I will, Father. I love you."

"And I you."

She tapped the End icon. After setting the alarm, she plugged her phone back into the charger and closed her eyes. Tomorrow was going to be a long day. In the meantime, she could dream about high cheekbones and soft smiles.

Her eyes sprung open. No. She was here to work hard and honor her father. Step four: make it right with her father. Check. Almost.

Her thoughts drifted back to Colin and she shook her head. She refused to get into some romantic entanglement.

But those cheekbones....

# Chapter Five

*I* wish we had Judge Judy in our corner."

Colin's muttering had been going on for the past fifteen minutes while pouring over documents she'd brought from Colorado, but that quiet statement almost made the peppermint mocha blow out her nose. "What?"

She'd never seen a man redden so fast. Ha!

"Uh...shoot. I said that out loud, didn't I?" He grimaced.

"Yuuuup."

Colin slid a finger between the collar of his shirt and his throat. "Well..."

She had to put the poor soul out of his misery. "That show is my guilty pleasure."

"It is?"

Li motioned an X across her heart. "Promise."

He laughed, the sound like melted butter, and she wanted to savor every moment of it.

*Blargh!* She shook her head. *Focus, Li.*

"So why Judge Judy?"

Colin looked up from a paper he was reading. "Because she has the funniest sayings. And because she's level-headed and no-nonsense. Unlike Darren the Hun."

This was too true, though she didn't know anything about this Darren "The Old Boss" Hun. She swallowed. "Are you sure you're okay with quitting your job?"

He snorted. "Even if I wasn't, it's too late now." He quirked a brow and eyed her. "But yeah. I'm more than okay with it. It's been a long time coming." Colin looked back down at the sheet. "Not looking forward to telling my parents, though."

She offered up a sympathetic smile. Oh, how she could relate to that one. Her parents had wanted her to go into medicine, but after she passed out dissecting a frog in her fifth-grade science class, they relented. After that, they pushed her to engineering, but her math...she slapped a hand over her mouth to stop the cackle. Engineering was a big no. During her teenage years, she fought them tooth and nail and her father, exasperated, threw his hands in the air and claimed she'd make a very good lawyer. Li took that to heart, though Father hadn't meant it as a compliment, and sat for law school. He wasn't the happiest with this choice because he knew how draining it was, but wasn't any career draining at some point?

"Earth to Li." Colin's hand waved across her face.

Oh! "Sorry. Just daydreaming."

He grinned. "Unfortunately, Mr. Fu can't win his company back on daydreaming."

Heat flamed her cheeks. "You're right. I'm sorry."

"Nah. It's no big deal, and this is a lot of info to take in and process without taking breaks." He scratched under his chin. "I'm thankful hostile takeovers don't often actually go through, but we really need to have our bases covered. Schultz will be pushing for this win, especially after he learns I'm assisting you."

Li stood and reached her arms towards the ceiling, glad they'd agreed to meet at the law library at Rainier University where she could dress down a little. She wished they could have met in a coffee shop so she could be even more comfortable in yoga pants and a sweatshirt. As it was, at least, she was able to wear stretchy jeans and a sweater. Cozy was good in the Seattle winter. "I think it's time for a break. My mind is a sieve right now. I can't seem to retain anything. Want to go get some lunch?"

Colin closed his laptop. "Food sounds good. So does coffee."

She peered at the shadows under his eyes. "Didn't sleep well?" It felt like she carried a load of bricks on her own shoulders.

"No, not really." He yawned. "Sorry. I didn't realize how tired I am."

"Totally understandable. Especially after your day yesterday. Do you need any help coming up with your next steps?"

"You mean steps other than telling my parents? I don't think so. Maybe. I'll probably need to sell all my belongings just to be able to make it back to Ohio." A grimace that may have been an attempt at a smile crossed his face. "Or you could pretend to be my girlfriend so when I tell my parents I'm moving back, they don't pester me about marrying their best friend's daughter."

Oh, little did he know how good at pretending she was. She bit down on the inside of her cheek. "I mean...if you think it would help."

Colin's eyes shot wide. "No! No, I was joking. Though I'm sure they'd be impressed that I'd been able to find someone so smart and..." His cheeks reddened. Seeing a man blush was something to behold. And it only made him better looking.

A Cheshire-cat grin spread her lips. "And...?" It was fun seeing him squirm.

"And—" he met her grin-for-grin. "And beautiful."

Heat creeped up her chest and neck. She slid her gaze to the law books piled on the table in front of her. "Thanks," she whispered.

The awkward silence filled the study room they occupied. So yeah. How to come back from that? What had they been talking about before they sidetracked? Oh! Food. Food was always a good tension breaker. She swallowed. "So," Li croaked, "about lunch?"

"Food! Good idea. I like food." Colin was about as smooth as she was. "Where to?"

"We could always just hit the student union since we're short on time to get prepared for our meeting with Futures."

He nodded. "Sounds good to me. I've heard their food here is great."

They shrugged into their coats and left the room. Colin swiped a key card to lock it behind him so their things wouldn't be disturbed. And swiped again. And a third time.

"This thing isn't locking."

"Want me to try?"

"I think there's something wrong with the card."

"You could—"

"Let me try again."

Li bit her lip and watched as he swiped two more times.

"The dumb thing."

"Well, if you—"

"Maybe I should run to the front and see if we can't get another one."

"I don't think it's necessary," she spat out before he could interrupt her again.

"But if It isn't working..."

"If it isn't working, you could try turning it around." Her chest hurt from holding back the laughter.

Colin flipped the card and swiped. Sure enough, the door clicked.

He faced Li, his face deadpanned.

She nodded, as if she were the Queen of England. "You're welcome."

As she laughed, she took a step back. She watched as Colin's eyes grew and everything started to drag by in slow motion. His mouth formed, as if he was about to say something that started with an L, and he reached out toward her.

Why?

Then she felt herself falling backward.

Oh. She'd forgotten the room they were using was at the top of a short flight of stairs. Well, this was fun.

"Ack!" Her arms flailed in the air, making it hard for Colin to grab her, but after what seemed like three trillion years— give or take—he finally grasped her hands and pulled her toward him.

Could she admit the resulting hug was worth it? Until he turned her away from the stairs and stepped back.

"Are you okay?"

"Other than my pride, I'm fine." She squeezed one eye shut and rubbed her face.

Step five: make a fool of herself. Check. And check and check and check.

Colin motioned over his shoulder with his thumb. "Well, the door's locked."

The wheezing laugh that escaped surprised them both. As if falling for him wasn't bad enough.

"Falling for me?"

Of course she'd thought out loud. "Just shoot me now, k?"

Smirking, he swept his arms towards the stairs. "Why don't we go?"

"Please."

She could swear she heard him chuckling behind her, but she decided to be the bigger person and ignore it. Maybe she'd picked up some of her father's pride. Li rolled her eyes. No doubt that was true.

They left the law library and made their way into the damp breeze roaming across campus. The student union wasn't too far of a walk, but with slush on the ground from the light snow and drizzle overnight, they picked their way carefully, hands pushed into pockets and faces down, watching where they stepped.

When they reached the building, Colin opened the door with a flourish and bowed. "After you, Miss."

Li's stomach flipped. She liked this playful man. Maybe they could keep in touch after this was all over and be friends. Reacting to his bow, she curtsied. "Why thank you, kind Sir."

A group of students exited. The two guys snickered while the girl with them slapped the arm of one and said, "Shut it. That's so romantic and sweet."

Uh-oh. Not what she wanted to portray. She was here to do a job and honor her father, not flirt with the competition-turned-ally. Li scooted past Colin, relieved to find the union crowded and loud. They likely wouldn't be able to hold a decent conversation here. *Thank you!*

Colin tilted his head to the side. "I'm grabbing a burger. Do you want one, or are you gonna find something else?"

She looked around at the food choices: a salad bar, taco bar, pizza, burgers, pasta, vegetarian, and...an ice cream bar? Oh, she was so hitting that station up after her meal. She deserved it after the almost-fall-Freudian-slip incident. "I think I'll go to the taco bar. Because tacos. Why don't I meet you by the drinks and we can find a table?"

He gave her a thumbs-up and turned away. She watched him for a moment. He seemed to be a good man. After all, who would walk away from an established law firm that many jockeyed to get into because of his conscience?

Colin Wen would. And did. Heat warmed her cheeks. She needed to pay attention to tacos, not men.

Mm. Tacos.

After standing in line and loading her plate with a bottle of water, two soft beef tacos, rice, and a way too big helping of guacamole and chips, Li spied Colin by the drinks and made her way over.

"I grabbed a table right there," he pointed to a table a few feet away.

She nodded and walked over, set her tray on the table, and went to pull her chair out...but there was no chair. Huh? Li turned to find Colin holding the chair, ready for her to sit and push her in.

Chivalry? She thought it was dead. But if it was dead, Colin was bringing it back to life. Like the living dead? Chivalry was a zombie. Who knew? The image of a big C with a gray, tattered h, i, v, a, l, r, and y walking on shuffling feet made her giggle.

*Rein it in, girl.*

"Thank you," she said as she sat. Colin pushed her chair a little closer to the table and sat down across from her.

As she'd hoped when they walked in, the union buzzed with conversation, laughter, and shouts across the area with people calling out to their friends—too loud for any real conversation. After his display of chivalry—Li snickered again—she regretted her earlier hope. Maybe she'd bring lunch tomorrow so they could stay in the library.

# Chapter

# Six

The buzz and slight movement of his phone caught his gaze. The notification on the lock screen showed an email...from Huang Li. Huh? He flicked his gaze up at her and back to his phone. Huang Li sat across from him. Had she emailed him something and it just now arrived? Not impossible, but highly unlikely.

"I just got an email." He waited, staring at her to see if she'd make a comment about it taking so long. She hadn't mentioned an email earlier, though.

"Okay..." Li's head tilted to one side, enough to tell him she didn't know what he was talking about, then she sipped her water.

"From you."

It was like a fountain burst forth from her lips. Maybe he should have waited until she'd swallowed. But he hadn't, and now he reaped the consequences. Water doused her plate, splashed his plate, and sprinkled his face.

She'd really just spit on him. There was no denying the woman had a powerful geyser for a mouth.

Li coughed, her eyes leaking tears. Was she choking? Or was she crying because she was embarrassed?

Her coloring face told him the answer. He jumped up and in one step, was behind her, slapping her back. Hopefully she wouldn't sue him for assault.

He hesitated before slapping her back one more time. If Judge Judy taught him anything, it was that people would sue over everything. Maybe Li would take him on Judge Judy for her case against him? He'd always wanted to sit in the audience during a taping, but never imagined until now that he could actually be a litigant. Being a defendant wasn't on his bucket list, but if he got to appear before that judge...

Li's hand waved in front of his face. "Colin? I asked if you're okay."

"What? Me? I'm fine! What about you?"

"You weren't answering me. I thought maybe I'd shocked you into muteness." She chewed on a nail. "I'm so sorry about that." Her gaze traveled down to his chest. He followed her eyes and saw the wet splotches on his polo shirt.

"No, totally okay. It's just water."

"Water that was in my mouth." She covered her face with her hands, her shoulders shaking. Was she crying?

"Li, honest. It's not a big deal. No need to cry."

When her shoulders shook harder, he began to wonder if she really was crying. He grabbed her left hand and pulled it away from her face.

Sure enough, she *was* crying. Hard enough for the tears from choking to turn into tears of laughter. With her hands removed and the silence from the students around them watching the matter unfold, he could hear her laugh.

Wow. Uh... The high-pitched wheeze stunned him, but not as much as when the snort sounded before more high-pitched wheezing. Colin tucked his lips between his teeth. He. Would. Not. Laugh. But then people around him began to snicker, and before he knew it, he was doubled over, laughing harder than he'd laughed in far too long.

It'd taken her far too long to get herself under control, but she couldn't dwell on that. Her laugh was embarrassing, but no matter how hard she'd tried to change it when she was younger, it always ended up as a wheeze-snort. She rolled her eyes heavenward. *You could have changed it, Lord. I would have been eternally grateful.* She waited for a moment, but as expected, no answer. At least not for her laugh. She eyed Colin and his phone. He'd obviously forgotten about the email—at least for now—and she was thankful. If he thought it was from her, her father must have emailed him. Maybe he thought she'd told Colin who she was. Her teeth clenched. *Sorry, Father. I'm afraid I've disappointed you again, even if you don't know it yet.*

"Here, I found something." Colin looked up from the text he'd been studying. "I wish Mr. Fu had implemented the stocks with differential voting rights, but—"

"Yeah, but. He didn't. So, what's our next best option?"

"Well, it's kind of controversial, but it just might work. The Poison Pill Defense."

"Wait...we're going to poison someone? I didn't sign up to be a murderer!"

Colin's groan filled the small room. "Don't worry. You won't be breaking the oath you took when you entered the Bar."

The sweat that had broken out on her upper lip dried. "Ohthankyou."

Straight, white teeth gleamed. "You're quite welcome." He turned the book he'd been reading and slid it toward her, pointing at a paragraph. "The Poison Pill Defense. We can have Mr. Fu and the board create a shareholder-rights plan. If anyone buys over a certain percentage of the shares, the board would issue new shares and allow the shareholders to buy them at a discount. It'll dilute the stake and make the takeover just about impossible without Futures IT's approval."

Duh! Why hadn't she thought of that? The mental slap to her forehead would have hurt if it was real. "Right! You think this will work?"

Colin nodded. "I do. When is our meeting with him?"

Li slid her phone open and tapped on the calendar. "Tomorrow at...one-thirty."

"I'll focus on some research to see what percentage we should suggest to Mr. Fu and the board if you want to start preparing what you can of the documents?"

She nodded and opened the program she used on her computer to draft documents. Out of the corner of her eye, she saw Colin glance at his phone. He wouldn't let himself get distracted by the email now, would he? Her eyelids slid shut as she shot a prayer to Jesus. *Please no. Not yet, Lord.*

❦

Colin eyed Li as she studied something on her laptop. Her cheeks looked a little pink. Was she hot? Winter in Seattle wasn't exactly like living in the Antarctic, but it wasn't warm, either. He felt fine, but then, his body kept a pretty regulated temperature.

He realized he wasn't hearing the click of keys, though Li's hands looked to be on the computer. Deep in thought, I guess.

The phone vibrated in his hand. Why was Darren the Hun calling? He swallowed past the ball in his throat and answered.

"Hello?"

The fact there was no response didn't faze him. Darren often used that tactic to try to intimidate his subordinates. It used to work on Colin, too well. Nope, not today.

"What do you need, Darren?"

"It's Mr. Schultz to you."

If he rolled his eyes any further back in his head, he was afraid they'd go missing. "Are you calling to cease the takeover?"

Li's head shot up to look at him, her dark eyes wide. He shook his head. He knew Darren and was sure that wasn't why he was calling. That man had too much pride to back down.

His former boss scoffed. "Please, no. I'm calling to inform you—and only because Futures' company policy requires it and I heard through the grapevine that you're now partnered with the attorney—" he sneered the word— "that there will be a board meeting on Christmas Eve. It will be the final determination. The board will vote on whether to accept or reject the takeover."

Colin's stomach flipped. Christmas Eve? "You'd really try to take away a man's lifetime of work on Christmas Eve?" His gaze met Li's, whose face paled.

"What better gift could I give my client than something they want?" He knew Schultz had skimmed the line on many things, but he didn't realize what a snake the man was.

*Forget Hun. We should be calling him Lucif...* The immediate conviction laid heavy on his shoulders. Shoot. *Sorry, Lord.* He knew there should be no "but's" when it came to seeking forgiveness.

"Darren—" Okay, maybe it wasn't kind to make a dig at him, Colin mentally shrugged. "I hope you change your mind. Mr. Fu's legacy is at stake, and he worked hard to build this company."

"My client doesn't care about legacy. It cares about the bottom line." What sounded like papers shuffled in the background. "Be prepared to lose, Wen." Click.

Colin stared at his phone, looking at the home screen wallpaper—a photo of the Christmas tree lighting at Westlake Park last year. Normally, he was a sucker for all things Christmas.

This might be the first Christmas in his life that he was dreading.

# Chapter Seven

Stepping out into the cold didn't seem to cool down Colin's temper. After he'd told her about the call with Darren the Hun, they'd agreed to head for dinner, then work in the lobby of Li's hotel for a few more hours. They needed a change of scenery.

"I know it's cold, but do you mind if we walk?"

"Nope. I need the exercise," she replied. Li zipped her white coat all the way to the top, tugged on a turquoise knit hat and gloves, and slung her bag over her shoulder. Around them, light flakes drifted down, illuminated by the lampposts in the common area. It would be the perfect night for a romantic stroll. *If I had any intentions, which, of course, I don't.* None. Zip.

Her gaze slid to the side and studied Colin's profile. *But oh, could I ever.*

"Hey Colin!"

A male voice called from her right. Colin squinted, then a smile cracked his face. The first since he hung up with Schultz.

"Garr!"

As the man inched closer, Li could see he was just in front of a pretty red-haired woman dressed in wide-leg pants and a belted black coat. The two men slapped each other's backs, then the man Colin named Garr stood back and slid his arm around the woman's waist.

"This is my girlfriend, Lia Walker. Lia, this is Colin. We met at church."

Colin shook Lia's hand then turned to Li. "Li, this is Garrison McGarville. Garr—and Lia—this is Huang Li, a lawyer from Denver I'm assisting on a case."

Li sighed. He was mostly right. She was a lawyer, from Denver, he was assisting her, and her name was Huang Li...but the missing "Na" bothered her more than she could admit. She forced a smile past the guilt and shook hands with the couple. "Nice to meet you."

Lia brightened. "We're on our way to dinner. Would you guys like to join us?"

She couldn't be sure, but Li thought she saw the light in Garrison's eyes dim a little. "Oh, we shouldn—"

"We'd love to. Where are you guys going?"

Obviously Colin wasn't paying attention to his friend's body language. Li's gaze drifted down to the pocket on Garr's coat where his hand was stuffed. It looked like he was fiddling with something in it. Something square, if the outline she could barely make out was any indication.

"Spinasse," Lia said. "I'm drooling at the thought of their Tajarin con burro e salvia."

"Their what now?" Must not be a place Colin frequented.

"Just trust me," Lia grinned. "It's expensive, but oh-so-worth it."

Expensive? With a square in his pocket and no real enthusiasm for having a friend join.

Oh. Oh, no. No, no, no. They couldn't join. "Col—"

"Yeah, sure! Why not celebrate my lack of work with an expensive meal with friends?"

He was being sarcastic, wasn't he?

"Li and I were going to walk to dinner somewhere, but Spinasse is a little far. Are you two taking the bus, or do you have a car we can hop a ride with you in?"

"Colin!"

He tipped his head toward her. "I thought you were hungry."

"Yes," she murmured, "but maybe they'd like to have dinner on their own."

Lia laid a hand on Li's arm. "No, really, we'd love to have you." She turned to Garr. "Wouldn't we?"

Garrison rubbed the back of his neck. "Yeah, of course."

"Great!" Lia locked arms with Garr and spoke over her shoulder. "We're parked over here."

Trailing behind them, Li tugged the back of Colin's coat. "I really don't think Garrison wants us there."

He shook his head. "Nah, of course he does. He said so himself. He wouldn't have if he didn't want us there."

Li wasn't so sure about that.

The dark wood tables and casing contrasted the cream walls, with what looked to be wrought-iron chandeliers hanging overhead. Against the far wall, a bar stood with windows looking into the kitchen behind it. Colin looked through and saw a chef cutting ribbons of homemade pasta.

Talk about mouth-watering.

They were seated at a table with two brown wood chairs, a white chair, and a red chair. Murmurs from the kitchen drifted out and the lighting glowed. He'd never been here, but from the smells alone, he knew he'd be back.

Beside him, Garr fingered his pocket and took a swallow big enough that Colin heard it. "You okay? You seem a little off."

Lia nodded. "I noticed, too." She reached a hand over the table and felt Garr's forehead. "You don't seem to have a fever, though."

Across from Colin, Li rolled her eyes. Her mouth moved, but he couldn't hear what she said.

"What was that, Li?"

"What was what?"

"I thought you said something."

"No."

"But I could have sworn..."

"I didn't say anything." She shook out the napkin in front of her and laid it on her lap. When she looked up, she narrowed her eyes, staring him down like he should be reading her mind.

He shrugged, causing Li to roll her eyes again. Women. He didn't get them.

After they gave their orders to their waiter, he placed tall white wine glasses in front of them, along with a white oval plate with two long breadsticks laying lengthwise and chunks of Italian bread placed on top, with their dinners soon following.

Heaven help him, he was going to die in Spinasse, because he never wanted to leave. Colin and Li both ordered the dish Lia had mentioned, and the pasta was cooked so perfectly, the flavor so heartwarming, he didn't want it to end.

It wasn't until they'd ordered dessert that he noticed Garr hadn't said one word throughout dinner. He elbowed his friend.

"Why so quiet?" Colin didn't expect the shot of pain in his shin. "Ow!"

He glared at Li. "What was that for?"

"Oops," she spoke through clenched teeth. "I didn't mean to kick you. Maybe you and I should go outside and check it out, make sure I didn't bruise you."

Huh? "I doubt you bruised me. Besides," he glanced through the windows looking out onto the street, "it's dark out there. We wouldn't be able to see anything."

"Then maybe the restroom."

Was she drunk? He examined her wine glass. Hm. Not even half the wine was gone, so unless she was super sensitive to alcohol, it couldn't be that. "You can't go in the men's restroom with me."

Her chin jutted. Was she trying to tell him something? If so, why didn't she just come out and say it?

"I..." Finally, Garr spoke. It was like the cat got his tongue. "I think Li is trying to give me and Lia some privacy for something." He glared at Colin. "She can obviously read situations very clearly."

"What did I do? Or not do?" He was clueless. Utterly clueless. How could he not have picked up on something his friend was putting out yet Li, who didn't know anything about Garrison, picked it up?

"I brought Lia here tonight because..."

Lia tilted her head, her eyebrows scrunched together. "Garr? What's up?"

The waiter approached the table and laid plates in front of each of them, setting Lia's down last. "Lemon yogurt cake with almond gelato for you, Signorina."

The round ball of gelato was coated with almond pieces and sat on a white sauce. The lemon yogurt cake placed beside it had a white drizzle over it, and in the middle...

Oh. Oh no. So that's what Li picked up on. He shot a look at Garr, who only had eyes for Lia, then he spied Li with one eyebrow raised and her lips in a flat line, as if to say, "You nerd. How did you not know?"

He hadn't talked to Garrison in a few weeks, and while he knew it was serious with Lia and suspected this would come soon, he thought maybe on Christmas, not before Christmas.

Lia gasped, her fingers spread across her neck. "Garr?" She reached her fingers to the dessert and grasped the circle of rose gold and pulled it from where it sat in the middle of the cake. The oval dark blue topaz was surrounded by milgrain beading and a half-halo of small diamonds on the top and bottom.

Garr cleared his throat and slid from his seat to the floor in front of Lia on one knee. He took the ring and held it between his pointer finger and thumb.

Colin heard a soft sigh from Li, whose eyes were glassy. With tears? Yeah. She was tearing up for two people she didn't know. He smiled.

"Lia, you crashed into my life unexpectedly—" she laughed— "and since that moment, I knew you were the one for me. You not only met my challenges head on," he winked, "but you rose to the occasion and issued your own dares."

Colin flicked his gaze to Li, who, despite not knowing their story, grinned from ear-to-ear.

"Will you dare to share your life with me? Follow God with me? And face any future challenges together with me? Will you marry me?"

Tears slid down Lia's cheeks, a wicked glint in her eyes. "I don't know..."

Garrison laughed. "I triple-dog dare you."

It was then Colin noticed the quiet restaurant as everyone waited to hear Lia's answer.

"You know I can't turn down a triple-dog dare," she laughed through her tears. "Yes! Yes, I'll marry you!"

Applause filled the room as Garr jumped up and grabbed Lia by the waist, placing a sound kiss on her lips.

Colin looked over to find Li watching him. His heart thumped against his chest.

# Chapter Eight

The pillow puffed up against her cheeks as she fell back onto the hotel bed. She loved a freshly made bed. So much. Especially after a long day followed by a fun evening.

She still couldn't believe Colin didn't pick up on Garrison's signals to leave them alone. Ha! But after it was all done, she was happy he hadn't. It was so sweet being able to watch their beginning start the process of switching to happily ever after.

Would that ever happen for her? She'd spent her whole life studying, reading, and studying some more in order to achieve her dreams. She'd never even really had a boyfriend. Dates, sure, but something steady and serious? No.

Li flopped onto her stomach and glared at the clock. 11:58PM. With all the excitement of Garrison and Lia's engagement, she and Colin didn't finish their work. He also hadn't checked his email.

She squeezed her eyes. For a lawyer, he really wasn't attached to his phone...something she was grateful for. Would it be possible that he'd delete the email without ever reading it?

One could only hope and pray. *God? Please?*

Outside her door, the elevator dinged, and voices murmured. She thought through everything she and Colin had to accomplish tomorrow before their meeting with Mr. Fu and groaned. It might be best to pull an all-nighter then hook herself up to a caffeine IV until their afternoon appointment.

Her mouth stretched wide and a yawn escaped. Then again, it might be beneficial to set up that IV right now.

She slipped her legs over the edge of the bed and pushed herself into a sitting position. Colin had mentioned a defense about poison, something she vaguely remembered from law school. Li stood, picked up her laptop from the desk, made a nest of the pillows on the bed, and sat back down, leaning against them. She opened the computer to a legal search engine and began to work, typing notes along the way.

Within three hours, she had a brief outlined, something she would give to the courts to reason why the court should decide on her plaintiff's side, if it became necessary, and had rehearsed an argument or two to share with Mr. Fu in the afternoon...and moved to the desk chair, back to the bed, to the floor, and to the desk chair again.

Exhaustion ripped her attention away without warning. She leaned, pushing the back of the chair further, and tipped her chin toward the ceiling, stretching her neck, arms, and pointing her toes. Covering her mouth for a yawn, she stood and faced the now messy bed, spying the fluffiest of the three pillows.

"Let me come to you, my pretty." Li straightened the papers and computer on the desk, snapped the light off, then flopped face-down onto the bed and scooted herself toward the pillow of her dreams.

Too bad that pillow of her dreams didn't lead her to actual dreams.

Li tossed for a few hours before she gave up. But she refused to call her insomnia "guilt." Nope.

No.

Uh-uh.

Okay, maybe.

Guilt, and anxiety over Colin finding out she wasn't who she'd led him to believe. "It's for a good reason" was on repeat in her soul.

So was "The road to hell is paved with good intentions."

Yowser.

The coffee pot on the TV stand called her name. Hotel coffee wasn't her preference, but when push came to shove, she'd take it. She rolled off the bed and looked in the mirror.

"Yikes!" While her hair was straight, its length meant she could get some serious bedhead sometimes. Apparently, it was possible even when she hadn't slept.

A hairbrush, shower, and coffee were for sure in order. And not necessarily *in* that order.

After a coffee she regretted—she'd have to remember this hotel didn't stock the greatest beans in the world—and a steaming shower, Li stepped out of the hotel and into a Lyft, giving Colin's address he'd sent her while she was getting ready. The winter weather slowed cars down, but the forty-something man in the car next to her was rocking out to some unheard melody with a deep bass, banging his steering wheel, bouncing in his seat, lips moving a mile a minute.

Either that, or he was having a seizure.

The light turned green, and her driver was off. Soon she reached a low building somewhere in the city. The drive had been a little long, but it was slow so she couldn't be too far from her hotel. After paying the driver, Li exited the car, bag in hand, and glanced at her phone. Apartment 118. She saw the buzzer pad next to the entrance, slid a finger down the buzzers until she found 118, and pushed the small white button.

"C'mon in."

A *bzzz* sounded along with a click as the lock disengaged. Li pulled the handle and walked inside.

For a building an attorney lived in, it was pretty nondescript. Beige tile floor was surrounded by beige walls. One wall had a bank of black mailboxes and another wall had an elevator door, but that was all that graced the foyer.

Li walked past the elevator to where a hallway ran perpendicular to the foyer. She glanced to her left then her right, where she saw a door opened. That must be Colin's. She turned in that direction and walked to the door. 118. She offered a quick knock before stepping over the threshold.

For a man who looked so put together and stylish, Colin's home sure...wasn't.

"Your face is louder than your voice."

Could she jump any higher? "You startled me."

Rich laughter rolled over her. "Probably because you were staring in shock at my awesome décor."

She grinned. "That's not what I'd call it." Li kicked off her shoes and went further into the apartment. "Stark" wouldn't begin to describe it. She bit her bottom lip and turned in a circle. "Um...so what do you call your décor style?" She turned to land her gaze on Colin's face. Were his ears turning pink?

Colin cleared his throat. "Well...minimalist?"

Li sputtered a laugh and looked over her right shoulder. White walls—understandable if he rented rather than owned—light hardwood floors, an old brown corduroy club chair...a *crate* for a coffee table. And that was it. She moved her head to look over her left shoulder. Ah, yes. That's right. There was a brass and brown TV tray leaning against the wall. She hadn't seen one of those since she'd helped Father clean out her grandmother's home after her death.

Wow.

"Hey Wen?"

The male voice calling from down the short hall had Li's hand fly to her chest.

"Yeah, Chicken boy?"

"'Chicken boy? Say that to my face, you limp noodle!'"

Their two laughs harmonized. But really. They were quoting...she couldn't put her finger on it, though it sounded familiar. She knew it was a quote from some movie.

A man with cool, rich umber skin dressed in black jeans with a black T-shirt and partially zipped up black hoodie, sporting a moustache that framed a smile showing a slight gap between his two front teeth rounded the corner. No. No, no, no, no, *no!* Her heart palpitated.

"Oh, you're here! Wait...L—"

"Hi!" She jumped forward and stuck out her hand. "I'm Huang Li. I'm an attorney out of Denver here for a corporate takeover. Colin is helping me." She was rambling but couldn't help herself. "He's been super helpful. So helpful. And you are?"

Positive all her teeth showing in her grin was giving her away to Colin, she kept her hand out anyway, hoping and praying Munro Shackham would understand her plea.

His hazel eyes studied her for a moment before he took her hand. "Hi," he said slowly. "I'm Munro Shackham. Uh...Mush, to my friends."

"Mush?" That's not what people called him in law school.

Behind her, Colin snorted. "A combo of his first and last name. Also, a reference to a very goofy dragon in a cartoon movie."

It took her a second to figure it out, but when she did...*go figure.* The fictional character and Munro's personalities matched way too perfectly. Time to take back control and figure out Munr—Mush's reason for being here.

"So how do you and Colin know each other?"

"Networking event. But because of my *astounding* knowledge of corporate law," he grinned and smacked Colin on the shoulder, "he asked me to join you guys for a bit to help you with the meeting today."

"Oh! Speaking of meeting," Li walked to the crate and laid her bag on it, unzipping the top. She pulled out the stack of papers she'd worked on all night. "I put this together, if you want to look it over." She glanced at Mush. "Corporate law isn't my thing, normally."

"I know."

Colin's brows furrowed. "How would you know?"

Munro's hooded eyes sprung wide open. "Uh...you know. She doesn't look like a corporate lawyer."

Li looked down at her yoga pants, long-sleeved T-shirt, and bare feet. Yeah, okay. She could understand that. Eying Colin, she said, "Well, I *did* bring a change of clothes for the meeting later."

He leveled a grin at her. "Good thinking."

Mush clapped his hands together. "Let's go forth!" Followed by a laugh that sounded like a machine gun sucking its bullets back in.

# Chapter Nine

Mr. Fu shuffled through the papers one last time before he looked up. "I find this acceptable. Thank you for your work." His gaze moved from Colin's to rest on Li's. "Please thank your father for me."

Her father? What did her father have to do with this? He spied her knee bouncing under the table again. He could understand her nerves, especially since corporate law wasn't her specialty, but she did well, and by now—the end of the meeting—she should have calmed down.

Women were complicated.

He stood and reached across the table to shake Mr. Fu's hand. "Thank you for allowing me to be part of this case, sir."

The older man took his hand, shook it once, and released it. "The honor is mine." He shook Li's then Mush's hand.

They sat and watched as Mr. Fu walked past the window of the restaurant and on down the sidewalk.

"I'll be right back." Li stood and headed toward the restroom.

Colin swiveled his head to pin Mush down with his gaze. "Has Li seemed off to you at all?"

His friend's face paled. "How would I know? I—I don't really know her." He ducked his head and muttered something under his breath.

"What was that?"

"What was what?"

"You just said something, but I didn't hear it."

"You're imagining things."

"Am not."

"Are too."

"Am not."

"Are too."

"Am—"

"You guys! Really?"

Colin turned to face Li. "This is normal for us." Her dark eyes held steady on him. It was really disconcerting. "What? It is."

She faced Mush, leveling her gaze at him. He just shrugged and grinned.

As she sat back at the table, she rolled her eyes. "I got a call while I was back there." She faced Colin. "We have a meeting set with Darren Schultz."

"Ugh. When?"

She swallowed. Hard. Then looked at her watch. That wasn't a good sign. He glanced at his own watch. Three o'clock.

"Four o'clock."

Mush spit out the water he'd just sipped. "What?"

Colin sighed with relief when the water landed back in Mush's glass rather than on his own face. "Of course, Darren the Hun would want to give as little notice as possible." He shook his head. "You told him no, right?"

Li looked everywhere but at him as she shifted in her seat. "With the successful meeting we'd just had with Mr. Fu..."

"Li..."

She cleared her throat and peeked at Mush.

Colin's chest tingled. *Aw, man.*

They stared at one another for a moment before Munro opened his mouth.

"'Let's go kick some Hunny buns! Yee-ha!'"

Leave it to Mush.

The lack of Christmas music as they waited to be called back to the conference room made an impression. She hadn't noticed it her first visit. Her nerves had been too strong. But the orchestral version of "You're the Inspiration" playing right now was giving her a headache. Li stretched her neck from side-to-side. It had to be after four o'clock by now. It'd taken her, Colin, and Munro almost a half-hour to go from the restaurant to Shiloh and Shultz. She was thankful for the wait, however. Every minute counted.

A *swish* announced the door leading to offices and the conference room opening.

"Mr. Schultz will see you now."

When they'd first walked in, Li expected the receptionist to at least smile at Colin considering he was a former coworker. Instead, her blank expression matched her blank voice. Li swore she'd looked just past her hair to avoid making eye contact.

"This is where I bow out, guys."

Colin halted and ran a hand through his hair. "Yeah, I guess you need to, huh? No sense in Hun seeing your face and calling your boss to complain."

"Especially on a 'vacation' day."

Li stepped forward and wrapped her free arm around Munro's neck, then leaned back. "Thanks for your help...Mush." With more than just figuring out a strategy.

He grinned, the gap between his teeth endearing. "Just remember: 'play nice with the other kids, unless, of course, one of the other kids wanna fight, then you have to kick the other kid's—'"

"We get it, Mush."

"'My little babies, off to destroy a Hun.'" That distinct laugh she remembered from law school followed them as they walked through the door.

A door that felt like the opening to their doom. Or a prison cell.

Snow fell outside the high-rise window. How she so badly wished she was down in a park back in Denver, sitting on a bench watching kids make snow angels. Instead, she sat beside Colin in a conference room at a large table with not only Darren Schultz there, but several other lawyers and paralegals. She couldn't get the scene from the movie Munro kept quoting out of her head. *Did you see those Huns? They popped out of the snow, like daisies!*

She cleared her throat to keep from giggling out loud. It didn't go unnoticed by her that she was much like the Chinese warrior girl from that movie. Only instead of men's armor, she wore a navy-colored woman's power suit and heels...and a hidden identity.

Across the table, Darren the Hun stared at Colin. It was unnerving how he hadn't blinked in at least a minute. Li side-eyed Colin. He was staring, unblinking, right back.

The testosterone was strong in this room. Time for a woman to take action.

"Th—"

"I don't know why you're bothering, Wen."

What a warm welcome.

A corner of Colin's mouth hitched up, but he stayed silent. That must be her cue. Let's see if she could get at least one full word out this time.

"Our client, Mr. Fu, will not be driven out of his company."

Darren turned his gaze on her. Yikes. It felt like flaming swords were trying to pierce her power suit.

"Is that so?"

Colin's half-smirk became a full-on smile. One that gave her confidence.

Li pulled a folder from her brown-leather bag. She'd only prepared five—one each for her, Colin, and Darren, leaving two just in case. Turned out she should have prepared seven. Why Darren felt the need to have four extra people in the room was beyond explanation.

Unless...unless he wasn't confident about this.

She gasped, drawing Colin's attention. That had to be it! *The Hun is nervous.*

"I wasn't expecting your 'army' to be so...robust." She raised her brows. "Frankly, I'm flattered."

Beside her, Colin examined his fingernails, but his lips pressed together and shoulders shaking told her what he thought of her comment.

Darren's glare narrowed. "You should be running scared."

She started shaking her head before he even finished. "No. No, I don't think so."

Li stood to pass two of the folders across the table, leaving one for her and Colin to share. Darren pulled one folder closer to him, leaving the others to reach for their own.

Rude.

As she sat, her chair squeaked. Darren looked up, a frown marring his otherwise—well, no. Not handsome. Not even distinguished. He ruined that when he opened his mouth to speak.

Li watched as the lawyers read what she, Colin, and Munro had prepared. She'd know when Darren got to their argument. A few minutes ought to do it.

"The Poison Pill Defense? Are you kidding me?"

Ah. He found it.

Out of the corner of her eye, she saw Colin glance at his smartwatch and tap the face. Keeping his hands under the table, gave her a thumbs-up.

She leaned back in her chair, a sigh escaping.

They'd done it.

Colin sat up straight in his chair. "Not kidding, H...Mr. Schultz. Not at all." He turned his face toward Li and tipped his head toward the Hun.

It'd be her pleasure.

"We just received word that Mr. Fu and his board have just approved a shareholder-rights plan. Being so experienced in corporate law, I'm sure you understand what this means?"

Oooh. She now understood what it looked like when people said someone's head was about to explode. It was fascinating. Darren's beet-red face turned to stone, his chin jutted out. The lawyers and paralegals sitting beside him shifted in their seats.

*I wonder if they'll get Christmas bonuses this year?*

"Get out." The Hun's clenched teeth indicated they probably wouldn't.

Somehow, his associates knew he was talking to them. They grabbed their things and scurried out of the conference room, not one of them looking back. She didn't blame them.

Darren the Hun was downright scary.

His hand slamming down on the table tossed her heart into her throat.

She and Colin could use their own army right about now. She glanced out the conference room window into the hall, catching the gazes of a man and woman as they walked by. *Any takers? No?* She didn't blame them.

Yes. Yes, actually, she did. Who would leave them alone with Darren, knowing he was a nefarious...Hun?

"You cost me!"

The hoarse, low-pitched yell made Li grab for Colin's hand.

"What?" Colin sat up straight in his chair. "You didn't think we could outthink you?"

Li leaned toward Colin and whispered out the side of her mouth. "Why are you baiting him?"

The infernal man just patted her arm, not once looking at her.

Darren grabbed the edge of the table with both hands, stood, and leaned across it. "This isn't over." He slammed his hands down on the table once more before he stalked out of the room, the thud of his footsteps echoing.

Li wiped her forehead with the sleeve of her jacket. "That went well."

Whether because she was truly funny or it was just from relief, Colin snorted. Snorted!

She chose to believe it was because she was funny.

It felt like forever before he was done. She should take her show on the road. He picked up the folders left on the table, slid them into her bag for her, and stood to face her, that half-smirk lifting his lips again.

Her stomach jolted, as if lightening had struck.

"I think we should go celebrate."

"We should?" Drat that squeak in her voice!

"Yeah." He walked to the door and bowed, sweeping his arm in a motion for her to walk through. "Let's talk to Mr. Fu then go have some fun."

"Colin!"

They turned toward the feminine voice calling out. A beautiful woman with long, chestnut-brown hair, brown eyes framed by tortoiseshell glasses, dressed in a light gray pantsuit strode toward them.

"Gen, how are you?"

Li looked between the two, then stepped back as the gorgeous brunette slung an arm around his neck and hugged him. Oh. The thought of him having a girlfriend hadn't even crossed her mind.

"I'm okay. It's boring here without you." She faced Li.

"Oh, sorry." Colin stepped beside Li and motioned toward Gen. "Li, this is Gen Pelt, a paralegal here. She was my lifesaver. Gen, this is Huang Li."

"Ahh. The one you quit for." Gen grinned and reached out a hand to shake.

"I didn't...well, that is, I was already..." Colin shoved a hand through his pompadour.

He was cute when he was flustered.

Li took Gen's hand. "It's so nice to meet you." She let her gaze drop to Gen's left hand. The relief she felt when a finger sparkled with gold and diamonds was almost embarrassing. She looked back up to meet Gen's gaze. A gaze filled with humor.

Oh boy. She ducked her head, studying her shoes, but not before Gen grinned at her.

"Darren is pretty angry."

The paralegal laughed. "You think? I'm pretty sure his head is about to explode. Or his heart. I've never seen him that red before."

"More like burgundy."

"Uh, Colin?"

Li looked up to watch as Gen's chin lifted and her gaze went past them. Colin glanced over his shoulder. "Oh." He took hold of Li's elbow. "We should go."

"That's a good idea, Wen. Run away."

Ooo. The Hun returned.

Colin ignored the jibe. "Let's go have some of that fun we were talking about."

He led her to the elevator and out of the building like he didn't have a care in the world.

# Chapter Ten

"One can't be in Seattle at Christmastime and *not* go to the Holiday Carousel." Colin grabbed Li's hand and pulled her through the crowd. Darkness and snow still fell, the lights from the festive atmosphere at Westlake Park causing the snowflakes to glint like little diamonds. A breeze from Elliott Bay brought a bit of a sting to the cold. Around them, Christmas music filled the air and kids laughed. Nearby, a mother rolled her eyes when her son spilled his hot chocolate and started crying.

As they reached the carousel, tinkling music played in time to the riders spinning round and round, up and down on the colorful horses attached to gold rope-like poles.

It was cheerful. And sweet. Not to mention surprising that Colin would bring her here.

And maybe a little romantic?

"You ready to do this?" Colin looked like a little boy about to eat a bag full of candy.

It was endearing.

"Let's go."

After the crowd stepped off the carousel, she and Colin climbed on.

"I call this one!" Li chose a white horse with a pinkish mane that was draped with yellow roses and had a floral bridle. Around its neck was tied a blue and white striped scarf.

"Well fine. I guess that leaves me no choice but to take this one."

"Ladies first, you know. Be polite."

Colin laughed as he swung a leg over the white horse with long, blue mane beside her. It had a fun red scarf with white paisley tied around its own neck.

The carousel started slowly, then picked up the pace. Lights and faces watching them blurred, but she kept her gaze on Colin's.

It was magical.

And cheesy. Oh, so cheesy.

She loved it.

He was a total sap, and he had no shame about it.

Colin's gaze never left Li's as they rode their horses. And he so badly wanted to lean over and kiss her. Would she welcome it?

Her eyes told him yes.

But he was known to be a dunce when it came to women and their signals.

After their victory this afternoon, he was on a high. It felt good to best Darren the Hun. It felt even better to be on the right side of helping a business owner. Not that he'd ever really destroyed any businesses before, but he was sure he hadn't helped them.

The Macy store's Star glinted off Li's long, ebony hair.

The sap in him had the lyrics of *True to Your Heart* by 98 Degrees running through his head.

Oh man. Mush would be turning around and singing *I'll Make a Man Out of You* to him. He grinned, watching as Li lifted her chin as he rose above her and grinned back at him.

If he timed it just right...

As she rose and his horse lowered, he leaned toward her, bridging the gap between them. His gaze didn't leave hers as she shifted on her horse...trying to get closer to him?

Aw yeah. Now was the time to go for it.

His eyes drifted closed as he puckered his lips, ready for his first feel of her mouth.

"Colin!" Her voice squeaked.

He opened his eyes, but it was too late. *Thud.*

"Ow!"

"Ouch."

He refused to look when he heard snickers behind them. Instead, he rubbed his forehead, squeezing his lids closed so he didn't have to watch as Li's nose wrinkled and she rubbed her chin.

He was not the smoothest man in the universe.

The ride came to a stop. Li climbed off her horse, her lips tucked between her teeth. Hiding them so he wouldn't take another shot? He didn't blame her.

He should watch *Hitch* again so he could take notes...on what *not* to do.

They walked in silence through the crowd. When they approached his car, he hit the button on the key fob, starting the engine so they wouldn't have to sit in a freezer.

He opened the door for Li, then walked around and climbed in on his side.

"So when do you leave?"

*And* that, *friends, is how to win friends and influence people.* Talk about foot in mouth disease.

"Oh. I, uh..."

"Not that I want you to leave."

Was it getting hot in here? He reached over to turn the heat down. It was hot. So hot.

Or was it just him?

He watched out of the corner of his eye as Li wiped a hand over her face. It must be hot.

He hoped.

"Well, now that Mr. Fu seems to be in the clear, I guess I can leave tomorrow."

That wasn't what he'd hoped for. "Oh."

Silence accompanied them the rest of the way to her hotel. When he pulled up, he put the car in park and twisted to face her.

"Is there anything we need to do before you leave?"

Her throat bobbed. "I don't think so." Her gaze shifted away from his. "I think there's something I should tell—"

The beep on his phone had horrible timing. "Hold on a sec." He pulled the phone out of his coat pocket and swiped his thumb across the screen.

What...?

# Chapter Eleven

A moment after Colin's phone buzzed, so did Li's. She pulled hers out of her bag and swiped her thumb.

Oh no. She shot a glance at Colin only to find him watching her, the skin between his eyebrows wrinkled.

"How does Mush have your number?"

A group text. *Munro Shackham, you are SO in trouble!* She and Munro had exchanged numbers in school. Despite that, they hadn't kept in touch, making it easy for her to forget he had it. "Well..." Her brain scrambled. Had he left them alone at some point? To go to the bathroom? Or make copies? Anything?

Shoot.

He seemed to be reading her mind. "No, I never left you two alone. And you guys introduced yourselves, so you've never met before. Right?"

"Um..."

He raised a brow, not letting her look away.

"We kind of," she swallowed. Hard.

"Kind of?"

"Kind of went to school together." She picked up the edge of her shirt, rubbing it between her thumb and pointer finger.

"But you didn't remember each other when you met at my place?"

This wasn't going so well.

"We—we did." She gulped. "Or at least I did."

No, Munro did, too. He'd almost called her by name.

Colin grimaced. "But why...?"

It felt like Santa was sitting on her chest. She turned her head to look out the front window. "I didn't want you to know we knew each other."

"Why not?" She heard the question in the lift of his voice.

She had to face him when she confessed. She still didn't know if he'd seen the email "she'd" sent him, or if he'd accidentally deleted it. Either way, she had to man up.

"Because I was afraid."

Colin huffed. "Spit it out, Li. Afraid of what? Me? Why would you be afraid of me?"

"Not afraid of you." *At least not of being harmed by you— more of being hated by you.* "Afraid you'd find out who I really am."

He dragged a hand down his face. "You aren't making sense."

She leaned her head against the window, the cold from outside feeling good against the heat of her shame.

"I'm not Huang Li."

A sound like the scrape of a credit card against ice on a car window came out of Colin's mouth.

"Colin?"

His eyes bulged in his reddened face. He coughed. "I'm fine. Just...choked on my saliva."

That took talent. She looked back out the front window.

"What do you mean you aren't Huang Li? And why have you been pretending to be Li...and why did Mush go along with it?"

"Technically I *am* Huang Li—"

His jaw clenched. "You aren't making sense. How can you not be Huang Li while *being* Huang Li?"

"Because," she swallowed so she didn't choke on her own saliva. "Because, I'm Huang Li Na."

"Oookay." He shook his head. "I still don't understand."

She filled her chest with air and pushed it out past her lips. "I'm Huang Li Na. My *father* is Huang Li." She glanced at him. His face was back to normal color. That was good. "You've been emailing with my father. He was supposed to be the one to work for Mr. Fu."

"You mean," she shifted to face Colin as he spoke, watching him hunch over the steering wheel, "you've been impersonating an attorney?" He shoved his hands through his hair. "Why? What were you thinking? Why would your dad allow that?"

"My father—"

"Never mind! I don't want to hear it. There's no excuse for lying."

"But Colin—"

"You should leave, Li *Na*," he sneered, "since this fight seems to be finished anyway, go home."

He reached across her lap and pulled her door handle, shoving it open with his fingertips.

"Goodbye. Have a nice flight."

Ouch. That was that, she supposed. But still... "Thank you for your help, Colin," she whispered. "I couldn't have done it without you."

"Yeah. Without me aiding and abetting a fraud." He stared out the front window, his face made of stone. "Thanks for that."

"What did you expect, léi lei?" Father's resigned voice wasn't what she'd hoped for when she reached her room and called him. "You lied. You were unethical."

Yep. His brand of comfort definitely had a sting. "I know, Father. But my intentions were good. I didn't want you to go without chemo for any longer than necessary."

Father sighed. "Again, that was my decision."

Li Na fell back on the bed. "I know. And I'm sorry. I did it because I love you."

"I know, daughter. And I love you." A soft click followed his words, ending their call.

Her body shook like an earthquake before tears escaped.

Coffee shops were a place you were supposed to go hang out with friends and have a laugh or two. Not confront them about their dishonesty. Steam McQueen was their favorite café to hang out at, with Steve McQueen memorabilia, including the motorcycle from *The Great Escape*, all over the place.

Mush sat across from him, studying his green tea.

"Look at me."

"No," he shook his head.

One would think an established lawyer would have the maturity level of at least a 14-year-old. "Look at me, Mush."

Instead his friend looked out the window.

"Mush!"

Finally, he turned to face him. "We need to work on your people skills."

"But you—never mind." Colin sat forward in his chair, arms resting against his knees and hands clasped. "Just tell me. Why didn't you say something about her?"

"I didn't know the full story, man. I went from the bathroom to your living room and there she was. She jumped in front of you and introduced herself. I didn't—and still don't—know why. But I figured she must have a good reason." He picked an invisible piece of lint from his jeans.

Colin sat back. "I can't believe she portrayed herself to be a lawyer."

"She *is* a lawyer."

"But she *isn't* the lawyer I thought I'd been talking to."

Mush waved a hand in front of his face. "Semantics."

He groaned. "Semantics? Impersonating an attorney isn't exactly ethical. The Bar wouldn't be happy to hear about it."

"You aren't going to tell them, are you?" Mush placed his cup on the low wood and iron table between them. "That could cost her."

"And she'd deserve it."

"I can't believe you mean that. Did she sign anything using her dad's name?"

He snorted. "You mean *forge*? No. She didn't forge any paperwork."

"Not even with Mr. Fu?"

Colin thought back then shook his head.

"Then she didn't *really* impersonate Huang Li." Mush sat back and grinned. "Problem solved."

"Are you kidding?"

"I don't see what the problem is. She flew in, told you she was Huang Li—which she is, she just left *Na* off—worked with you to problem solve a potential hostile takeover, went *with you* to advise a client about a possible solution, then went *with you* to deliver the great news to the Hun, all the while not putting her name on anything." He lifted his hands in the air. "So, what's the problem?"

"I almost kissed her."

"Whoa!" He scooted the club chair he sat in closer. "Do tell. Why *almost*?"

Colin squeezed his eyes shut. "*Almost* because her horse rose while mine lowered and my forehead hit her chin."

For once Mush was speechless.

But only for a moment.

"I don't even want to know."

"Good. Because I'm not a 'kiss and tell' kind of person anyway."

"You *didn't* kiss her, Dude. That's the problem."

If only punching someone wasn't technically assault.

"So where is she today?"

Colin frowned. "Flying home."

Mush bolted straight up. "What? Why?"

"Because her work is done?" Sometimes he wondered about his friend.

"But *yours* isn't."

He shook his head. "I don't know about you."

"I don't know about *you*. You're really dumb."

What was there to say to that? He blinked.

"I felt the attraction between you two the moment I walked into your living room. You almost kissed her. And now you're letting her go because she added 'Na' to her name?"

When he put it like that.... "She lied. What don't you get?"

Mush lifted his gaze heavenward and muttered under his breath. "If Li Na lied, and if she's the same woman I remember from law school, then she had a good reason. You need to go talk to her."

He was probably right. The woman he'd spent the last few days with didn't reconcile to a deceitful person. She was smart, funny, a bit clumsy, but beautiful.

"You have the dumbest grin on your face. Get a hold of yourself, man."

Colin laughed. "Yeah, fine. I'll go talk to her."

"Good. Now I can drink my green tea in peace." He waved Colin off. "Go forth, young protégé."

If he was Mush's protégé, the world was in trouble.

"You're coming with me."

"I am?"

"You helped contribute to this mess, so yeah. You are."

Mush jetted his arm toward the door. "To battle for love!"

"You're pushing it."

He paused, looked back at Colin, then faced the door again, his arm once more reaching forward. "To battle for like!"

Colin dropped his shoulders, shaking his head. This friend was one weird character.

# Chapter Twelve

Please remove belts, shoes, and empty your pockets. All electronics, change, cell phones, and purses need to go in a bin." The TSA agents were on repeat.

How dull.

Well, until they got to do pat downs. But even then... Li Na shivered. No thank you.

The line at SeaTac was long...and young. No doubt all the college students heading home for Christmas. She groaned. That meant the plane would be full, leaving her with little chance of getting on the soonest flight out. Flying standby was no picnic and went against everything in her Type A personality, but when she tried to get her return ticket changed to an earlier flight, this was the best the ticket agent could do. She didn't want to stay in Seattle when there was no reason to, so... She let the thought drop and focused on her surroundings instead.

SeaTac was festive, with its live music playing. She even spotted some reindeer when she first entered.

Bah-humbug.

She loved Christmas, really. But while she was happy for Mr. Fu that Futures IT seemed secure, she'd spent the night tossing and turning over her deceit with Colin.

And Mush. She really owed him an apology, too, for forcing him into it all.

The crowd around her began to crescendo, kids squealed. Li Na turned to spot costumed Christmas characters in a parade marching toward security.

Sweet. Now if she could figure out a way to avoid them.

She should have brought ear plugs.

As the parade stomped by, handing out candy canes to pleading hands and tired parents, Santa Claus ho-ho-hoed in the rear. She flicked a gaze in his direction, but her eyes went right past him to...

The Hun? What was he doing here? Maybe going back home for Christmas? Though he didn't seem the type. She would have thought he'd stay in his office through all the festivities, working.

Li turned before he could spot her, and shuffled forward, following the line.

"Huang Li Na!"

Glancing over her shoulder, her eyes widened. Colin?

She scanned the crowd but didn't see him. Then a voice called her name again.

Li's heart jumped in her throat. Was Darren calling her name? No. He didn't know her full name. Unless Colin had told him. But why would he do that? He didn't work for Shiloh and Schultz anymore.

This was crazy. She knew she'd heard her name. She just hoped Darren wasn't paying attention and didn't hear.

Grabbing her suitcase, Li Na stepped out of the line. She hoped she wouldn't regret that. Security lines would only get longer. She pulled her hair over her left shoulder and bent her head toward the floor so her hair could form a curtain and hide her face from Darren.

"Li Na!"

Shoot. She had to get somewhere behind Darren so she could look through the crowd to see who was calling her. It sounded like Colin, but she was so short, she couldn't see over all the heads.

The line moved forward again as she walked past, a little too close for comfort to the Hun who was, thankfully, studying his phone. He didn't seem to be listening to anything.

Spying a bench, she whispered an apology to the airport cleaning staff and climbed up. At least now she could see over some of the heads.

Why did God make her so short?

She faced the direction she'd last heard the voice come from. And there he was.

Wait.

Make that they. Colin and Munro bobbed up and down on their toes. "Li Na!"

Should she yell out? She glanced in Darren's direction. He'd moved forward again but wasn't looking at his phone anymore. Still too close for comfort. Instead, she lifted a hand in the air and waved.

Mush spotted her and nudged Colin, who easily found her gaze. His smile was half-hearted, but she didn't blame him. She jumped off the bench, picked up her suitcase, and headed in their direction.

When she reached the men, she stopped, staring into the most expressive eyes she'd ever seen. Then she looked at Colin.

*Kidding!* His eyes were the only ones she wanted to look into.

It was enough to make her want to gag.

"Hi."

Behind Colin, Munro stuck his finger in his mouth. She laughed.

"Hi," she answered. She focused back on Colin. "What are you doing here?"

"I realized I didn't really give you a chance to explain." He made a fist, sticking his thumb out and over his shoulder. "This goof made some valid points this morning, so I figured I better come talk to you before you left."

"Mush, you are the wisest—"

"And fiercest. And don't forget hot. I may have been known to singe a woman or two."

"Go home, Mush."

"Ain't no one appreciate me around here."

Li leaned to the side to speak to him. "Go home, Mush."

"Yeah, that's what I'm talkin' about. No appreciation. Even when I find his phone," he pointed at Colin, "with an email from 'you,'" he pointed to Li Na, "and realize it's from your father, so delete it."

Colin's jaw dropped. "You *what*?"

So that's what had happened to the email Colin had received in the law library. He must have forgotten all about it. She mouthed, "Thank you" to Mush.

Mush grinned, tipped his head, and left the two of them standing in the middle of the Christmas crowd.

"Why would he delete an email from you?"

She waved a hand between them. "It wasn't important." She swallowed. She'd tell him about it one day. Soon, because she was done being dishonest with Colin. But right now, there were other things to work through.

"So."

"Yeah." She shuffled her feet. "So."

"Do you, uh...want to go get coffee?"

"Make it hot chocolate, and you've got a deal."

He grimaced. "I don't know about you."

"Are you kidding me? You're the one who took advice from Mush."

His eyes crinkled. "Yeah, you've got a point. I'll leave you to your flight then. Bye."

Li Na grabbed his arm before he could walk away. "Oh no you don't. You came here for an explanation, and you aren't leaving without one." She looked over her shoulder at the security line. Darren the Hun was looking around the crowd. Time to vacate this place. "Besides, don't look now, but the Hun is here. We need to move before he sees us."

"No way he's here. It's Christmas. He's probably locked up in his lair, working."

"Now isn't the time to not believe me. I don't know about you, but I don't want another encounter with that man." She took hold of his hand and tugged both him and her suitcase toward the exit.

"Where are you parked?"

"Parked?" He whacked his forehead. "Mush drove. We'll need to find an Uber."

It took a few minutes, but the line of people waiting for a ride dwindled and they hopped in a black sedan. Colin named a café and the driver shot away from the curb.

Once they reached the coffee shop, Colin paid the driver and helped Li from the car. He took her suitcase into the shop while she trailed behind him.

They placed their order and found two seats at a small table. As they sat, Colin watched her. Better now than never. She took a deep breath.

"My father is sick."

"I'm sorry to hear that."

Li shook her head. "No, I better start from the beginning."

She explained her father's friendship to Mr. Fu, how she made off with the plane ticket, then made Colin promise to keep her father's illness to himself.

"Whoa, I'm sorry." Colin reached across the table and covered her hand with his. "I don't blame you for stepping in. Waiting on chemotherapy isn't something that should be done, even if just for a few days. This takeover could have taken weeks."

"Knowing my father, he probably was already thinking of the Poison Pill Defense and could have had it finished up within a few hours, but I still didn't want to risk it." She swallowed past the lump in her throat.

"Have you talked to your dad since you left?"

She grabbed the napkin in front of her and started shredding it. "Yeah. He wasn't happy."

"But you did it with good intentions."

"And we all know where the road of good intentions leads."

Colin smiled then rubbed the back of his neck. "Li...Na." He looked up at her. "I'm not the best-versed in Chinese. What does your name mean?"

She grinned. "Nothing that even closely resembles me. 'Elegant.'"

"Hm."

Hm? What was that supposed to mean? She watched as he studied her.

"I think it fits you rather perfectly."

Oh. That's what that was supposed to mean. Her stomach flipped.

If he wasn't Don Quixote, he didn't know who was. He was as smooth as melted butter. Aw, yeah. Mush would be proud.

He also meant it. She wasn't just pretty, though, she was beautiful. And the more he got to know her, the more beautiful she became. As for elegant...well, her looks were elegant. Physically, she was a bit of a klutz. He snickered. It just drew him to her that much more.

Li rummaged through her bag and pulled her phone out. She swiped across with her thumb, then spent a minute tapping away. He watched as her hair swayed with her movement. She looked up to find him staring.

He grinned. No shame in getting caught admiring someone.

Her answering smile was soft. The next words, however, felt like a brick slamming against his chest.

"The next flight is in three hours. I should get back to the airport."

Right. She didn't live in Seattle.

"Oh."

They sat watching each other, not even noticing the barista swiping their empty mugs away.

Li stood and shouldered her bag. "Well. I suppose this is it. For real this time."

He wiped his hand down his jeans then stood facing her. "Yeah. I guess."

Colin so badly wanted to grasp her hand as they walked to the exit. She stopped in the doorway, looking out toward the street. Her exhaled breath formed clouds lighter in color than the ones in the sky producing ice-cold rain. He rolled his neck.

And spotted a miracle.

*Don Quixote, eat your heart out.*

"Uh, Li?"

He pointed up when she looked over her shoulder.

Her eyes lifted, following the line of his finger. Straight above her hung a twig of mistletoe. With a grin, he stepped forward, standing as close as he dared. Her chin tipped up with her lips slightly parted. An invitation?

Colin lifted his hand and cupped her cheek. "I've wanted to do this for so long." He bent toward her, watching as her eyes drifted shut.

The most wonderful time of the year, indeed. Even the screeching of the bus engine coming toward them didn't faze him.

It wasn't until the bus passed and a *whoosh* a millisecond before dirty, freezing cold puddle water doused them.

Er...doused *her*. She acted as his shield.

Who said chivalry was dead?

# Chapter

# Thirteen

*L*i stood there in front of the man she thought might be from her dreams, still as a statue, gray-brown water dripping down her arms and back.

*Ugh.*

Colin's wide eyes stared at her, as if she'd not just grown a second head, but the head of a unicorn.

She pressed her lips together, trying hard to hold it in.

Yeah, it was no use.

First, a snort, then a bark, then she was bent over, holding her stomach as she totally and completely lost it. She heard her own wheezes, but it only made it worse. She didn't even care that people were staring. That *Colin* was staring.

She was dead. *Dead.*

There were worse ways to die than from laughter, though.

The barista, with his hair in dreadlocks and a scruffy goatee, scurried over to her, a small white towel clutched in his hand.

"Here," he thrust it at her.

Li took it, half wondering what she would do with a tea towel, laughing even harder at the absurdity of it all.

"Let me." Colin's eyes sparkled with suppressed laughter—hopefully at the situation and not her. He grasped her shoulders and turned her so her back faced him. She felt the towel wrap around her hair, his hands gently squeezing.

Laughing didn't seem so appropriate anymore.

Could this be the most romantic thing she'd ever had done for her?

Scratch that. The *only* romantic thing ever done for her. *The woes of studying too hard and not dating.*

She'd been missing out.

"There you are."

And completely missed the rest of Colin's tending. *Blargh!*

"Thanks," she turned back to him. "I should go change my clothes before heading to the airport."

Dreadlock-guy still stood there, watching them with a grin. He stuck this thumb over his shoulder. "The bathroom is back there."

Li nodded. "Thank you." She wiped off the hard, plastic shell of her carry-on, then pulled it behind her, Colin following.

"I'll wait outside the door and order an Uber while you change."

"You're the best." She reached the door and pushed.

After locking the door, she laid her suitcase on the counter and dug through her clothes. Most of them were dirty, but she knew there was a clean pair of black leggings in there somewhere. And a long sweatshirt.

Bingo!

Fighting to get her soaked skinny jeans off, she leaned against the counter and tugged until she was free, standing on top of her shoes so she didn't have to put her feet directly on the bathroom floor.

A tap on the door sounded. "You okay in there?"

Could any girl be okay when trying to take off wet skinny jeans? "Just fine. Thanks."

She balled the jeans up and put them in a bag she'd brought for dirty clothes. Whipping the leggings through the air, she straightened and turned them to face the right direction.

Ew. Her legs were cold. And wet.

Unless she was in the shower, she hated being wet. She looked around for a paper towel dispenser, but only found an electric hand dryer. Shoot. But it was worth a shot.

She depressed the large silver button. A loud roar echoed through the small bathroom. Now how to dry the back of her legs?

She grasped the edge of the counter with her hands and lifted her leg out behind her.

"Everything okay in there?"

"Fine."

How did figure skaters do it? It wasn't a comfortable position, especially when standing on top of her shoes to avoid touching the floor.

Heat from the dryer barely reached her calf. Ugh. She straightened. If it didn't work for the leg closest to the heater, it wouldn't work for the other leg. So, she'd have to suck it up and put her leggings on while she was still wet.

Li turned to lean against the sink. Sticking her foot into the first leg, it got caught. The fabric was sticking to her. She grunted.

This was going to be fun.

"Li Na? It sounds like you're being beaten in there. Are you sure you're okay?"

She rolled her eyes. "Don't worry about me."

It took a minute, but she finally got her foot through the leg hole. Now for the other one.

This is where things took a dive.

Balancing on the foot already through the leg hole and on her tennis shoe, she leaned back on the counter and lifted her right foot. She hadn't given enough thought to standing on one shoe on a floor wet from her dripping clothes.

Li barely caught herself as she fell forward.

Hello, close call!

Hm. How to do this?

Colin knocked on the door again. "The Uber should be here in five."

"Okay, thanks," she called.

She decided to jump up and sit on the counter, though it wasn't big. Still balancing on one foot, she turned herself to face her suitcase, zipped it closed, and sat it on the floor. Ew. But that's what Chlorox wipes were for.

She twisted again and hopped up on the counter. There was barely enough room for her, but she could make it work. Surely her behind wasn't as big as her suitcase.

She eyed the rectangle piece sitting on the floor. It was like it was mocking her. Maybe her behind *was* as big. She'd have to start doing squats when she got home.

It was a precarious position, but she pulled her right leg up so her heel barely rested on the counter, and leaned forward to stretch the opening of her leggings. Her foot slid through the hole just fine.

*Thank you!*

Unfortunately, the rest of her leg was still too wet. She struggled to pull the leggings up but couldn't get a good enough grasp. She rested her hands on the counter beside her, lifted and scooted herself back a little further, the faucet pushing into her tailbone.

The sink cupping her behind wasn't the most comfortable position she'd ever been in, so she hopped off the counter onto her shoes and started wiggling.

"Li, are you sure you're okay? You sound...I don't know."

"I'm *fine.*"

Men had no clue what women went through.

She felt like she was a Kung Fu master trying to get the leggings pulled up. Her treading leg, front, side, and reverse kicks really made it. She giggled.

Li quickly exchanged her shirt for the sweatshirt, ran her fingers through her hair to detangle it, not bothering to look in the mirror. She knew she was a mess. After slipping her shoes back on, she stepped through the door as Colin's phone buzzed.

"The Uber just arrived. Perfect timing." He looked up, but his gaze didn't get past her shirt. His lips parted as his brows dipped low. Then he sputtered. And guffawed—that was the only word she could think of to describe what he was doing. Guffawed.

It wasn't until he pointed that she remembered what her sweatshirt looked like.

Could the earth please open up and swallow her now?

The long red sweatshirt wouldn't have been an issue...but it had Spock on the front in his blue shirt wearing a red Santa hat—with a 3-D pom-pom at the end and white trip on the rim. Beside him were three giant snowflakes, and below the words "Trek the Halls" were in glittery gold and green.

Obviously, her mind was elsewhere when she pulled it out of the carry-on. She had big regrets not looking in the mirror before she left the relative safety of the bathroom.

"I never would have pegged you for a Trekkie."

"I'm no—oh, never mind. Yes, I am. I'm a die-hard Trekkie. Get over it." She grinned. It was fun seeing him laugh. Even if she *was* the root cause.

Step six: leave on a good note. Check.

Colin grabbed her suitcase from her and headed to the exit. She followed. Begrudgingly.

Outside, the rain had slowed to a drizzle. The driver, a woman probably in her late 20s, got out and popped the trunk. Li watched as Colin put the luggage in.

This was it.

"So, this is it," Colin echoed her thoughts.

She slid her tongue over her top lip. "Yeah, I guess."

"Well..."

"I should..."

Li spoke again. "I should get going. That security line at SeaTac won't get any smaller."

Colin pursed his lips and nodded. "Yeah." He leaned in and wrapped his arms around her. "Take care of yourself, Huang Li Na," he whispered.

She swallowed past the lump. There was no way she should be this attached to someone she'd only known a few days. "You too."

He opened the passenger door for her. Once she was in and buckled, he said a quiet "Goodbye," then closed the door on what had likely been her most favorite week in years.

# Chapter Fourteen

It was déjà vu, but instead of watching the Space Needle as she flew in, she watched thousands of lights on buildings across the landscape as they descended.

This time the flight crew didn't make any funny announcements or crack jokes with the travelers. It was like they sensed her mood and wanted to leave her alone to mope.

Or it could have been that it was just late and everyone was tired. Either or.

What she hadn't expected was to see her father at the baggage area.

"Father? What are you doing here?" He looked worn. Wrinkles she'd never noticed before were pronounced around his eyes and mouth. It had only been a week, but it looked like he'd aged fifteen years.

"I came for my daughter."

She wrapped her arms around him. As short as she was, he was just as height-challenged. Her father would only come up to Colin's chin.

Shaking her head to rid herself thoughts of Colin, she said, "But I have my car here. And it's late. You shouldn't have driven."

"I didn't. Sharlene—" Ah, the next-door neighbor she suspected had a crush on her father— "showed me how to call for...uh..."

"A taxi?" If he couldn't remember that word, he was worse off than she'd thought.

"No, no. That wasn't it."

Huh. Oh, but would her dad really go for it? "An Uber?"

He snapped his fingers. "Yes. An Uber." He tipped his head to the side. "Though what the difference is between an Uber and a taxi, I don't think I'll ever understand."

He had a point.

They walked to the shuttle that would take them to the Economy East parking. The relatively short walk was made shorter by the shuttle, something she knew her father would appreciate. And if she were honest with herself, she did, too. Who wanted to walk in the Denver winter at ten o'clock at night?

Flying standby wasn't something she would likely do again. She couldn't handle the uncertainty. As it was, she was the only fortunate one who got on the flight out of Seattle to Denver via Salt Lake City. She hoped the other two people flying standby to Denver made it out.

After finding her Rav4—thank goodness for smartphones and the airport's website that helps you remember exactly where you parked—she stored her luggage in the back, helped her father into the passenger seat, and climbed in, blasting the heat.

"So léi lei. Jian called and told me about his meeting with you and this...Colin?"

She held her breath and nodded. He may not be able to see her, however, so she answered. "Yes. Colin Wen."

"He liked him. And you. He said you made a good team, knowledgeable."

"Thank you, Father." She smiled. "It was mostly Colin. He's an excellent attorney."

"As are you, léi lei. Do not diminish yourself."

She slowed to a stop at a traffic light and rested her hand on top of his. "I love you."

"And I you."

Stretching her arm, she slammed her hand on her phone and tapped to snooze the alarm. It was way too early. She groaned as the backup alarm blared *Reveille*. She'd chosen it because she figured if it helped soldiers get up and going in the mornings, it would help her.

It didn't.

The aroma of brewed coffee drifted under her door and met her glee. Okay. She could get up for coffee. She didn't drink it every day, but she loved a good cup of joe when she'd been up late, and her father made some of the best.

After she showered and dressed, she made her way to the tiny kitchen. Living with her father at her age wasn't exactly a moment of pride for her, but she'd started law school a little later than some and needed a free place to live. Now with her dad having cancer, it was a good thing she was there.

"Good morning."

"'Morning, Father." And that was as much as they'd talk until they each finished their caffeine intake. Li Na grabbed her favorite mug from the cupboard—her white "Good morning, I see the assassins have failed" mug—and poured the black liquid. She added the cream and sugar, toasted a bagel, and sat down at the table for two. The house was older, small, but it reminded her of her mother. The kitchen's cornflower blue wallpaper with tiny white daisies warmed her. Mom had been so excited to put the paper up over twenty years ago after living with yellow-painted walls since she'd married Father. The off-white laminate cupboards and countertop were showing their age.

"It might be time for an upgrade to this kitchen." She looked at her father to see his reaction.

He eyed the space critically, then shook his head. "No. Not yet. Let us see what happens with my health. Besides," he paused. "It is like a hug from your mother every time I come in here."

Hello punch to the gut.

They drank their coffee in silence until the doorbell rang. Startled, Li Na jumped in her chair and caught her father's gaze. "Are you expecting someone?"

"No." He glanced at his watch. "Especially not this early." He moved as if to stand.

"I'll get it."

She jumped up and made her way to the door. When she opened it, her stomach jumped in her throat.

"What are you doing here?"

# $\mathscr{C}$hapter
# $\mathscr{F}$ifteen

$\mathscr{I}$s that any way to greet someone?"

If snakes could speak, they would sound like Darren Schultz.

Li stepped through the door and closed it behind her, wrapping her arms around her stomach to ward off the chill. "How did you find me?"

The Hun smirked. "Mr. Fu was kind enough to pass me your phone number. And I'm a lawyer. It didn't take long to find you." He tilted his head to look through the living room window.

She moved into his line of sight. "And *why* would you want to find me? The matter is at rest."

"Oh," his voice slithered over her. "The takeover is at rest, for now. There's another matter I've found out about."

Sweat broke out on her upper lip despite the cold. Dare she even ask?

"And that would be...?"

"You, my dear, are not who you said you were."

Busted.

"I think it's best if I come in, don't you?"

The door opened behind her. "Léi lei, invite him in."

Li looked behind her to see her father smiling. He must not realize who this is.

"Father, I don't think—"

"Do not be rude, Daughter."

Her stomach dropped from her throat down to her feet. She bowed her head. "Yes, Father." She turned to face the Hun. "Please come in."

Darren smirked as he walked past her. "Don't mind if I do."

"Would you like some coffee or tea?" Leave it to her dad to be polite to a reptile about to go for the strike.

"I don't think I'll be staying long." Darren eyed Li Na. "After you left the office with my old whipping boy," he sneered, "I looked you up. And found both you *and* your father. How convenient."

"And your point?" She should take lessons on kindness from her father. But today was not that day.

"You misrepresented yourself, missy."

Father's shoulders jutted back as he stepped closer to the Hun. "You do not speak to my daughter in that way, especially in my home. You bring dishonor to your family."

"You think I care, old man?" He cackled. "No. I don't. What I *do* care about is getting my client what they want: Futures IT. So," he faced Li Na. "You will call your client up and have him and his board back down. Everything can proceed on the 24th, as it should."

"No way."

He raised his brows. "Then I'll have no choice but to report you to the bar."

"That's blackmail!"

Who knew snakes had shoulders to shrug? But shrug he did. "Call it what you want. You're the one who crossed a line." He grinned. "First."

He walked to the door, grabbed the handle, and opened it, allowing a gust of cold air to blow in. "If Fu doesn't back down on Tuesday, expect to be reported." He walked out, not bothering to close the door behind him.

Li slammed the door and turned to face her father. "Daddy..."

He spread his arms, and she flew into them, wrapped in his warmth and love.

"I'm telling you, you need to talk to her."

"What's the point? She lives in Denver. I live in Seattle."

Colin held the cell between his ear and shoulder as he worked on the laptop, reaching out to contacts at all the law firms he could think of in the Seattle area.

"You do realize people have been in long-distance relationships before, right? And that they've worked?"

"Name one."

"You're kidding. Adam and Becky? Okinawa and Vancouver?"

Mush had a point. "Yeah, I forgot about them."

"How? They only met in person three times, and the third was their wedding."

"And they're an anomaly."

"No, they aren't."

"Yes, they are."

"No, they aren—"

"Enough, Mush. I'm not in the mood."

"Killjoy."

"What are we, eight?"

"Give or take."

Colin sighed. "Whatever. Just...I should go. I need to get more resumes out."

"Wish my boss would hire you, man."

"Me too." So did his bank account. He had a substantial amount in savings, thanks to full-ride scholarships so he could avoid student loans, but he hated digging into it.

"Catch you at the White Elephant party?"

Oh right. "Where's it at again?"

"Grant and Lyndsey booked Steam McQueen."

"What time?"

"Six."

"I'll be there."

"Don't forget the $20 limit."

"Will do."

After ending the call, Colin sat back in his chair, his laptop changing to a screensaver on the crate. He thought of Adam and Becky. Maybe he and Li Na *could* work it out.

But he was getting ahead of himself. He knew she was at least attracted to him, but he didn't have a clue whether she was actually interested.

His watch buzzed. Tapping on it, he saw the reminder for the meeting with Mr. Fu, his board, and the Hun—along with Li Na, if she showed—on Tuesday. Christmas Eve.

She probably thought the meeting wouldn't happen since the Board had agreed to the defense. No doubt she was right, but he'd called his parents to cancel Christmas with them. The parental unit hadn't been pleased, but if the meeting happened, he wouldn't be able to get home unless he took a red eye and arrived in Ohio in the very early morning. And that was if he could even get a flight.

Resumes flew out into cyberspace the rest of the afternoon. Around three o'clock, the game and wrapping paper he'd ordered online arrived. Thank goodness for two-hour delivery.

He wrapped the White Elephant gift and went to get ready, praying he'd hear back from one of the law firms he'd reached out to. With it being two days before Christmas, he doubted it, but miracles never ceased.

He walked through the door of Steam McQueen right on time. Grant and Lyndsey, Mush, and a few others were already there. Lyn had gone all out decorating the place for Christmas.

"Hey you guys."

"Hi!" Lyndsey squeezed him from the side and took off. She was a riot. As introverted as possible, but you wouldn't find anyone kinder.

"You made it," Grant approached from behind. "So glad to see you."

"I almost didn't. I'd totally forgotten until Mush mentioned it earlier today." He lifted the gift. "Where should I put this?"

Grant pointed to a table on the other side of the shop. "Right there."

The bell over the door—the one with the mistletoe hanging over it—tinkled. "Go get a drink and some food and find a seat. I'll talk to you in a bit."

As introverted as Lyndsey was, Grant was the opposite. They were so perfectly suited for one another.

Colin dropped the gift on the table and went to find a caffeine fix.

They were deep in the gift exchange, fighting over the black tie with Guy Fieri's face all over it and the Star Wars tiki mug. The *Wheel of Fortune* game he'd brought sat in the lap of a happy Mush. He should have known his friend would hang onto that game for dear life. He had an unhealthy obsession with the game show. Colin was still shaking his head over the gift he'd scored: a white T-shirt with John Travolta's name across the top...and Nicholas Cage's face pictured below. A tribute to the movie *Face-Off*.

The bell over the door rang, but his friends were so loud he might be the only one to hear it. He turned to see who'd come in. Grant and Lyn had rented the space, but it was dark out now, so someone may not have seen the "Closed for Event" sign posted. He hated to disappoint whomever was hoping for a good coffee, but—

"Li Na?"

A quick glance around the group showed only Mush had noticed. His eyebrows popped up, creasing his forehead. His gaze flew to Colin. He shrugged. He had no idea why Li Na was back in Seattle.

He rose to meet her by the door.

"I didn't mean to interrupt. I didn't even know you'd be here."

"No, it's okay. Friends rented the café for their annual Christmas party."

Laughter erupted behind them.

"Score!"

Colin glanced over his shoulder. "Looks like Grant got the tie."

"Tie?"

He grinned at Li Na. "Let's not even go there."

"Hey you two!" Grant ran over to them and stuck his hand out to Li Na. "I'm Grant. You joining us?"

"Oh," her face pinked. "No. I didn't realize there was a party going on." She took Grant's hand. "I'm Li Na."

"Ahhhhh." Grant nodded slowly, a grin spreading his mouth. "I've heard about you."

"You have?" Colin laughed when they both spoke at the same time. "Poke, poke, you owe me a Coke."

Li rolled her eyes. "Hello, nine-year-old Colin."

Grant shoved his shoulder. "I like her." He faced Li Na. "We bring a couple of extra gifts each year in case this happens, so you really need to join us."

"What is it?"

Colin answered. "A White Elephant. Where you choose a gift or steal someone else's."

"Oh! Dirty Santa!" She grinned. "I do love a cutthroat game."

Mush yelled from the group. "Bring it on!"

Li Na stood on her tip toes to see Mush. Her eyes widened. "Oh, game *on*! I want that, Munro Shackham."

"What?" Mush's face fell. Ha! Wait...she wanted the *Wheel of Fortune* game?

*Star Trek* and *Wheel of Fortune*? She was one weird individual. No wonder she and Mush got along so well.

What did that say about him?

That he had great taste.

# Chapter

# Sixteen

Li Na couldn't remember the last time she'd laughed this hard. Colin and Mush's group of friends were hysterical.

She hugged the game to her chest and grinned at Mush. "Sorry...nah, no I'm not. Not at all."

He pouted across the circle from her, staring at the emoji Chia Pet in his lap. "Not cool, girl. Not cool."

"Hey, I got the game, so *very* cool."

"You're a cruel, cruel woman." He peered at Colin. "You sure about this one?"

Beside her, Colin choked on his hot chocolate, sputtering droplets on his lap. "Dude."

She had no idea what they were talking about, but whatever it was, it had Colin flustered.

It was too adorable.

Colin wiped his jeans with a napkin, side-eyeing her. "What are you doing here, anyway? Not that I'm not happy to see you."

Ooph! She'd almost forgotten her reason for being back in Seattle.

Well, her professional reason, at least.

"The meeting with Mr. Fu and the Hun."

"What about it?"

She pushed her lips out. She really didn't want to tell him, but she was determined to not hold anything back from him, especially after being dishonest about who she was.

"Darren Schultz came to my house in Denver."

"What?" His raised voice brought the conversation around them to a screeching halt. She felt heat creep up her neck and into her cheeks.

Colin waved a hand. "Sorry, everyone. No biggie. But my colleague and I need to talk work, so we're going to get going."

*Colleague?* Her body weighted down, as if a semi-truck full of bricks parked on her.

They said their goodbyes, Li Na thanking Grant and Lyndsey for welcoming her and providing a gift so she could join the game. She found the woman who'd received the gift, a beautiful blond with deep brown eyes. Colin said her name was Story. Definitely a unique name, but it suited her. So did the gift she'd ended up with: a cream macramé woven wall hanging. It seemed like Lyndsey had put a lot of thought into the extra gifts, like maybe she'd be giving them to others. And maybe this particular gift was meant for Story anyway.

Li Na smiled. She loved it when friends were thoughtful and knew others so well.

"Ready to go?"

Jolted out of her thoughts, she glanced at Colin. Her *colleague*. Dejected, she replied, "Yeah. Ready."

He quirked a brow in question, but she ignored him, gathered her coat and carry on, and followed him into the brisk

night air.

"Where are you staying?" Colin pressed the Start button of his Passat and turned the heat on full blast.

"Um, I hadn't even given it any thought."

What? "You flew out to Seattle two days before Christmas without knowing where you're going to stay?" Come to think of it, he was surprised she'd even found a ticket.

Li Na bit down on the corner of her bottom lip. "Yeah. I had something else on my mind." She pulled in a deep breath. "The Hun knows about me."

"Yee-aaah. Of course he does. He's met you."

"No, I mean *me*. And my father."

"You mean..." Oh. "How did he figure that out? Not that it matters. What did he say? Do?"

"What did he threaten, is more like it."

"He *what*?" His hands balled into fists. If he'd hurt Li Na....

"He said if I didn't talk Mr. Fu and his board out of the Poison Pill, he would report me to the bar."

His pulse sped up. "That weasel."

"He isn't wrong, Colin. I was unethical at best."

Twisting his body, he faced her. "Okay, yeah. It wasn't the wisest thing to do," he admitted, "but as Mush pointed out, you didn't *really* misrepresent yourself. Your name was the same—mostly—and you didn't sign any paperwork, right?"

Her eyes lowered, she nodded.

"Then the worst would, should, be a reprimand. But I don't think the bar would even do that." He slid a finger under her chin and tilted her face up to see his. "It'll be okay."

"You don't know that."

She was right. He didn't. "No, but we can pray about it together."

She squeezed her eyes shut, but he saw the glistening before she did.

Grasping her hands in his, he started. "Lord, thank You for this woman and her heart to serve and protect her father. We just want to ask for Your protection on her and her status with the bar. Please be with us," he felt her twitch, "as we go into that meeting tomorrow. We know it's right for Mr. Fu to keep his business, so please give us wisdom and courage to honor You."

He stopped, wondering if Li would pray.

She didn't disappoint.

With a quiet voice at first, it grew in strength. "God, I was so wrong. Wrong to dishonor my father by going in his place and pulling the wool over the eyes of everyone I came into contact with. Wrong to dishonor You by being deceitful. Please forgive me. And like Colin, I ask for wisdom and courage to honor You tomorrow, and to stand up for what's right in this battle."

"Amen."

Their fingers entwined, they stared at one another.

"So."

"So."

She scrunched her nose. "I guess I should find a hotel."

As she said that, Lyndsey tapped the window. When Colin lowered it, she grinned.

"You guys okay? It doesn't sound like you're having car trouble."

"No," Li Na said, "we were just talking and praying."

"And about to go in search of a hotel."

Lyndsey's head tipped to the side, her golden-brown hair following. "You don't live here?"

"Oh, no. I live in Denver. I just arrived here and thought I'd come get a coffee. I hadn't even given any thought to where I'd stay."

A shot of wind blew past Lyndsey into the car. "Forget a hotel. We have a spare bedroom." She stood and called over her shoulder. "Grant, Li Na is going to stay with us."

"Okay," he waved as he slid into their SUV.

"Are you sure? I'll be flying back home tomorrow night, but I don't want to be a burden."

"Psh. No burden. You can ride with us, if you'd like, that way Colin doesn't need to trek out to the 'burbs."

He should have known his friends would offer up their home for Li Na, but the air felt heavy in his lungs.

Li Na turned to him. "It would be easier for you." She didn't quite meet his gaze.

"I can pick you up tomorrow morning for the meeting, then take you to the airport."

"Are you sure?"

No. He wanted her to stay. Her father, however, probably wouldn't be enthused about that idea. "I'm sure."

Finally, her eyes met his. "Thanks," she whispered before she tugged the door handle and stood out of the car. He followed, opened the trunk, and pulled her carry on out, taking it to the Baker's vehicle.

When she'd buckled up, he closed the door, waving as they pulled away from the curb.

# Chapter Seventeen

"It was my fault, Mr. Fu. I'm so sorry for putting you in this position." Li Na blinked back tears. It did no good to anyone if she did what she wanted and fell to the floor in a blubbering mess.

She was *not* a pretty crier.

The man standing in front of her carried a load on his shoulders. He sighed. "Ah, Li Na. I forgive you." He took her hand in his. "We all make mistakes."

"Thank you so much, Mr. Fu."

"Now," he pushed his hands together and rubbed, "I must speak with the board and instruct them to withdraw the shareholder offer."

"What? No!" Her head felt like it was floating. "No, please don't."

"Mr. Fu," Colin interjected, "she's right. Please don't."

Li Na glanced at the man standing confidently beside her.

"But if I do not, Mr. Schultz will report her."

She and Colin had been in the reserved room at the King County Courthouse since mid-morning, talking through their approach for the upcoming meeting. The clock hanging on the beige wall ticked the minutes away, like a harbinger of doom. What doom? The Hun.

Colin's voice brought her back to the problem at hand.

"—and because of that, the worst she would likely face is a reprimand. I don't think she'd even have that."

Mr. Fu's gaze shifted between them, as if he was trying to ascertain the truth of it all. She nodded. "I spoke with my father and he agreed. It wasn't the wisest decision on my part, but it isn't the end of the world."

"I must admit, I am relieved."

*You and me both.*

"I think it's safe to say we all are," Colin breathed. He turned to Li Na. "Are you ready to face the Hun?"

"The Hun?" Mr. Fu's brows lowered over his eyes.

Umm...whoops. Mr. Fu was traditional and appreciated respect, both received and shown to others. "We, uh..." Colin stammered.

Her turn to be *his* knight in shining armor. "I apologize, Mr. Fu. It's just an inside joke."

"Ah," he spoke as if he understood but it was clear he didn't. That was okay, as long as he didn't realize they really *were* disrespecting Schultz.

Talk about feeling convicted. But would they stop calling him Hun?

Yeah, probably not.

"Mr. Fu, may I serve you more tea?"

"That would be wonderful."

Li Na picked up the cup that sat in front of him on the table for six in the middle of the room then opened a tea bag and poured hot water from the Keurig on the counter. When she sat the cup in front of him, he tapped two fingers on the table, an indication of his thanks.

"When are we expecting Mr. Schultz?" The Board's vice chair, Ms. Benson, pursed her thin lips.

Colin glanced at the clock on the wall above Mr. Fu's head. "Five minutes ago."

Mr. Fu grunted. Darren "The Hun" Schultz wasn't winning brownie points.

Li Na sat at the table and shuffled papers around. She swigged some water from the bottle in the table in front of her. She crossed, then uncrossed, her legs. Bounced her knee. Looked up at the clock.

One more minute had passed.

The windowless office was getting to her. If Schultz didn't show up soon, she was going to scream.

The ticking knocked another minute off the clock.

Mr. Fu sat straight in his seat, occasionally sipping at his tea. Ms. Benson tapped away on her phone. Colin sat beside her, drumming his fingers on his knee.

"I should have brought my new board game."

Colin smirked. Mr. Fu's eyes brightened. "Oh, I love board games. What is it you should have brought?"

Thinking out loud was probably her greatest nemesis. "Um, *Wheel of Fortune.*"

"*Wheel of Fortune* is my favorite game. And I love *Jeopardy!* too. It is too bad you do not have the game here."

"It would definitely help pass the time."

Several more minutes passed in silence before voices were heard outside the door. Finally.

Li Na straightened in the chair, she and Colin bookending Mr. Fu and Ms. Benson, facing the door. As it opened, she and Colin stood. Mr. Fu and Ms. Benson followed their lead.

Darren Schultz stepped across the threshold, his chest puffed out. Behind him followed one of the lawyers she'd seen in the boardroom at their previous meeting, and...Gen Pelt. She glanced down the length of the table at Colin, who raised an eyebrow when he saw his friend. Li Na flicked her gaze back to the woman who watched her, the corners of her lips lifted. Then she winked. *Winked.*

That was a good sign, right?

Gen must be nervous. Her tick only showed itself when she was stressed. Colin hoped that didn't portend bad things.

"Good afternoon, Mr. Fu." The Hun then deigned to rest his gaze on Li Na then Colin. How kind. "I trust we're here to do the right thing."

"That we are, Mr. Schultz," Mr. Fu answered.

Everyone sat in the uncomfortable, generic office chairs.

"I've had my paralegal, G..." he looked at Gen with a blank stare.

Had he forgotten her name? It wouldn't surprise him.

He turned back to Li Na. "I've had her draw up the papers for this business transaction."

Mr. Fu placed his hands flat on the table and pushed himself to stand. He glanced at Li Na and Colin, then said, "No."

Hun's brows lifted. "No?"

Li Na stood beside Mr. Fu. "You heard him."

The chair protested as Darren leaned back and steepled his hands in front of his chin. "You do realize what this means for you, Huang Li *Na*, yes?"

Both Colin and Ms. Benson stood. The churning of blood in his veins was deafening to his own ears, but Colin refused to acknowledge Hun's not-so-veiled threat.

In his peripheral vision, Colin watched Gen's eye wink again where she sat on Schultz's left side. That tick must be really bothering her today.

It was when both her eyes winked that he really paid attention to Gen. He swept his gaze to directly meet hers. If he hadn't been watching carefully, he would have missed the flash of her smile.

So it *wasn't* a twitch. What was she getting at?

Down the row, Li Na cleared her throat. "Mr. Schultz, I do understand what you're getting at, as does my client."

Colin leaned forward to see past Ms. Benson and Mr. Fu. He wanted to watch this fierce woman in action.

She raised her chin. "I'm not threatened by your blackmail."

Across from her, Darren frowned, but remained silent.

"As a matter of fact, I've been in contact with the Bar."

She had? His stomach flipped.

"You have nothing to talk to the Bar about when it comes to me."

He eyed Schultz. Interesting that he would think she talked to the Association about *him*. Sounded like Li Na hit a sensitive spot.

The knock on the door didn't break Li Na's eye contact with the Hun. As it opened, Colin saw a face appear.

Mush?

His friend's wide grin proudly displayed the gap between his two front teeth. As Mush walked behind him toward Li Na, Colin heard his friend's infamous rat-a-tat-tat laugh under his breath.

This was about to get good.

Mush leaned close Li Na and said something, handed her a file, and sat down beside her. Pointing to Schultz, he said, "Ooo, you about to get cooked."

Li shoved a hand over Mush's mouth. Yeah. Probably a good idea.

"Mr. Schultz, two things. One, I was in contact with the Bar about my actions."

Well, that toned down the smirk on his face.

"I don't owe you an explanation of what they said or what, if anything, they're going to do to discipline me, but suffice it to say, they're aware."

Discipline? That didn't sound promising, but the load taken off Colin's shoulders felt good. He was proud of her for doing the right thing, despite what may happen.

"Two, I did talk to them about you."

Schultz sat up in his chair. "About what? You have nothing on me."

What was that cliché? *If looks could kill.* Li Na would be dead a thousand times over. A little defensive, maybe?

The woman stepping out of his dreams and into reality held up the file Mush gave her. "I beg to differ." She opened the folder and began reading. "Confidentiality violations." She looked up at the Hun. "Tsk."

Gen was very intent on studying her fingernails. Interesting.

"'Borrowing' client funds."

Colin watched Darren's face as it deepened in color.

"Inflating attorney fees."

This was the man he'd been working for? He knew Darren was shady, but this was downright awful.

"Would you like me to continue?" How did Li Na know all this?

Darren jumped up from his chair. "You have no proof of this!"

Li Na's relaxed posture spread peace down the line on their side of the table. Colin glanced at Gen. She also looked at peace. She caught Colin's gaze and winked.

No, no tick there today. *Ah. So* that's *how Li Na found out.* He grinned.

"'Now that's what I call Mongolian barbecue.'"

And once again, leave it to Mush.

# Chapter Eighteen

The snow falling on the Denver street was the perfect end to a near-perfect day. Li Na glanced over her shoulder and watched Father as he napped in his recliner. She'd paid a fortune for the return ticket to Seattle for yesterday's courthouse showdown, but it'd been worth it in order to be back here to spend Christmas Day with him.

"I am proud of you, léi lei."

"You're supposed to be sleeping."

"How can I sleep when pride is expanding my chest so far my buttons might pop?"

"And how can you have pride when I brought dishonor to our family?"

Father opened his eyes and pushed the handle of his recliner forward, bringing the chair to an upright position. "I was harsh with you, and for that, I ask your forgiveness. I know you only wanted to protect me. My pride can get the better of me, can it not?"

She wasn't going to touch that question with a ten-foot pole. "Father, it's me who should be asking forgiveness. I should have talked with you before doing something so dumb. Please...forgive me?"

He held out his arms and she rose, rushing to him. He had his own battle in front of him but she'd brushed up on her warrior skills and intended to fight alongside him. Cancer wouldn't win.

The Huangs would.

The tiny kitchen didn't afford much room to cook a large Christmas dinner, but her father wasn't all that hungry anyway. Still, she couldn't let the holiday go by without their traditional meal of Peking duck, pork and cabbage dumplings, cold sesame noodles, and Father's favorite, almond cookies.

As she brushed each cookie on the sheet with a beaten egg, the doorbell rang. "I'll get it, Father." She hummed along to *White Christmas* as she slid the cookie sheet into the oven, wiped her hands on a towel, and headed for the door. The Christmas tree she passed barely reached the top of her head, but the multi-colored lights always made it feel larger than life. She glanced as a ceramic ornament with her mother's photo on it and grinned. She physically missed her, but her presence was thick in this home, especially on a holiday that meant so much to Mom.

The doorbell rang again, and she picked up her pace. It was odd someone would be here on the night of Christmas Day, but maybe it was Sharlene dropping off something for Father. She flung the door open with a singsong, "Merry Christmas!"

"Merry Christmas to you, too."

It was like he'd walked right out of her dreams. His dark eyes reflected the lights from the tree in the living room. She stood there, gaping. It was a good thing flies weren't around in winter or she'd probably have swallowed three or four of them, with her mouth wide open like that.

"Colin? What are you doing here?"

His hands were stuffed inside the pockets of his black winter coat. "Freezing." He shivered.

Yes, he was. Oh! "Come in, please."

He stepped through the door and past her. As she closed the door behind her, she asked, "Can I take your coat?"

"Thanks." He unzipped and shrugged out of it, then turned to face her father. He stuck out his hand. "Hello, Sir. I'm Colin Wen."

"Ah, yes. I've heard much about you. I owe you thanks for helping my daughter and friend."

"It was my pleasure." He turned to Li Na with a smile on his lips.

It was so hard to breathe when he looked at her like that. She grasped for words. "So...really...what brings you here? On Christmas Day? If you were going to travel anywhere, I would have thought you'd go home to Ohio."

"Please don't tell my parents," he laughed. "They'd kill me." He ducked his head. "I just wanted to come see how you're doing."

But... "I just left yesterday." Were those butterflies dancing in her stomach?

"Yeah, but. Well. I, uh," he ran a hand over his hair and down the back of his neck. "I didn't get to say everything I wanted to before you left."

"You didn't?"

"No."

She waited but he didn't say anything else. "What was it you wanted to say?"

"Uh...well..."

Time to take pity on the man. She grinned and pointed a finger in the air. She watched as Colin's gaze followed her finger up toward the ceiling...

...Where a sprig of mistletoe hung over his head. A slow smile widened his mouth. He moved his eyes to look back at her. "Ah."

She shrugged. Who was she to break Christmas traditions?

Standing on her tip-toes, she leaned in and placed her hands on Colin's chest. He bent his head, and with his lips hovering just over hers, whispered, "Merry Christmas, Li Na."

She touched her lips to his. She was home. "Merry Christmas, Colin."

Step seven: Find the man she didn't know she'd been dreaming of. Check.

When their kiss ended, Colin leaned his forehead against hers. There were things to figure out about their relationship and the distance between them, but that was a question for tomorrow.

Tonight? Tonight was made for celebrating. "Would you like to stay for dinner?"

From behind, her father spoke. "Would you like to stay forever?"

# Epilogue

Colin held the phone up, recording the moment. He refused to admit he was crying, but...it was allergies. Yeah. That was it.

Allergies.

Through the phone's camera, he watched as Li Na stood beside her Father, tears rolling down her face. She wasn't kidding when she claimed to be an ugly crier, but those tears were well-deserved. On his other side, Sharlene stood, her own tears flowing as she held Li's free hand.

He was so happy for those two.

Huang Li pulled the rope dangling from the bell three times. As a normally stoic man, he was trying his best to hold back his own emotions. But hey...when a person reached the end of his chemotherapy treatments, it was good to feel gratitude and joy.

It'd been a long year of two courses of chemo for Li, and just as long a year for Li Na as she cared for him. But he hoped this marked a new chapter. In all their lives.

Colin fingered the gift inside his pocket. He couldn't wait to give Li Na her Christmas gift.

His stomach rolled. Then again...

She caught his gaze and smiled, her eyes showing her own joy—and relief—at her Father's restored health.

This was going to be a good Christmas.

"So? Is tonight the night?"

Colin watched Li Na at the kitchen sink, drying dishes beside Sharlene, who was washing them. He turned to Li and nodded. "With your permission, Sir."

"You do not need my permission, Colin. But you do have my blessing." He laid a frail hand on Colin's. "Even that you do not need, as long as Li Na loves you. And I believe she does."

Colin turned back to Li Na. Yeah. He believed she did, too.

The woman of his dreams glanced over her shoulder and grinned at him.

The nausea that'd been prevalent in his stomach all day finally dissipated at her smile, replaced with a racing pulse and spike of adrenaline.

"Li Na?"

She turned, a wet plate in her hand.

He tipped his head toward the living room. She set the plate on the counter and followed him in.

"I have a gift for you."

Li and Sharlene entered the room. "Colin."

Uh-oh. Was her father changing his mind? "Yes?"

"I first have a gift for you. If you would like it, that is."

Sharlene handed him a large, white envelope she'd been holding behind her back. Li shuffled toward Colin and Li Na where they stood by the tree and held it out. "Please," he nodded. "Open it."

Colin slid a finger under the flap, breaking the seal, and pulled out the sheaf of papers inside.

A contract? Was Li going to demand a bride price or something? He glanced up, but all eyes were on him. Li Na's head tilted to the side, a half-smile on her full lips. Her father stood with his shoulders back, watching him. Sharlene, the petite white-haired woman at Huang Li's side, had a full grin on her face.

He bent his head to read the contract.

"Partnership?" His gaze flew to Li's. "You're offering me partnership in your law practice?"

Li Na gasped and grabbed the papers from his hand to read for herself. "Father? Really?"

Li nodded. "If you are willing, I would be honored to have you as a partner."

Colin's heart thudded. "Sir. I'm floored. And *I'm* the honored one." He met Li Na's gaze. "But I have my own question first."

He lowered himself, one knee on the brown carpet, and took Li Na's left hand. Her right hand flew to her mouth and tears brimmed her eyes.

"Last Christmas, you asked if I would like to stay for dinner. Your father," he glanced in his direction with a grin before meeting Li Na's eyes again, "asked if I'd like to stay forever."

He couldn't help himself. He leaned forward to kiss Li Na's hand, her skin soft beneath his lips.

"This Christmas, I would like to ask you the same thing. Huang Li Na, will you stay with me forever? Will you marry me?"

She pressed her lips between her teeth, the brimming tears now falling down her cheeks. Then she gasped. "Yes! Yes, I'll marry you." She took his face between her hands and bent down to place her mouth on his.

When she stood, she pulled him up beside her. Colin turned to face her father. "Sir, I would be honored to be your partner in your practice. Thank you."

He turned back to Li Na, raising his eyes to the ceiling. "Ah, the great mistletoe." He grinned at her. "We better not break tradition."

Step one: fall in love with the woman of his dreams, a fierce, beautiful, loyal, loving woman, and have her love him back.

Check.

## The End

# Acknowledgments

As always, first and foremost, Jesus gets the praise. This story was harder than I thought it would be to write, and it's only because of Him and His grace that it happened.

Mark, once again, thank you for your patience as I worked through cooking dinners, leaving it to you to cook. It's a good thing you don't burn food like I do. Thank you for your love, encouragement, support, and care. You amaze me.

Van and Ellie, you two are the best kids. Ethan and Ashlyn, you too. I love all four of you deeply. You all bring me so much joy. It's an honor to be your mum/mum-in-law!

Toni, Andrea, Jaycee, and Angela, thank you for including me in this collection! What an honor. Even more, I appreciate your friendship. You ladies are amazing! And so fun!!

Toni, you know by now that you lent your name to Shiloh and Schultz. Yeah. Um...thanks for that. Ha! Gen Van Pelt, thanks for lending *your* name, too...even though you weren't aware that you did so. My bad. ;)

Lyndsey, thank you, sweet friend, for your input, help, encouragement, and opening your home after the tornado so I could have electricity to get this story done! And Grant...thanks for peeking in the window to make sure I was working. LOL!! I hope you two enjoy being a little part of this story!

Jadon, Anike, Autumn, and Clara, you guys are so loved!! You're amazing kids whose love for Jesus teaches me so much. I can't wait to write you, Van, and Ellie into the story we've all planned!

And to you, dear reader: Out of all the stories you could have read, thank you for choosing this one. The notes I get from you do so much good for my heart! I truly appreciate the time you take out of your life to spend with me and my characters.

And just so you know...Bo and Story are *finally* starting to open up a little about their story! Caprice is sharing hers, too. So be on the lookout for their full-length novels! If you don't know who I'm talking about, I'd love for you to go back to the beginning and read about Tyler and Allegra in *Count Me In*.

If you enjoyed Colin and Li Na's story, I would so appreciate if it you head over to Amazon and Goodreads to leave a review! Even if it's just one very short sentence like "I loved it!" You'd make this author cry. A good cry. Though I warn you, I'm an ugly crier.

Mikal Dawn is an inspirational romance author, wedding enthusiast, and proud military wife. By day, she works as an administrative assistant for an international ministry organization, serves in her church, runs her kids to figure skating and rock climbing, and drinks lots of coffee. By night, she pulls her hair out, wrestling with characters and muttering under her breath as she attempts to write. And drinks lots of coffee. When she isn't writing about faith, fun, and forever, she is obsessively scouring Pinterest (with coffee in hand, of course!) for wedding ideas for her characters.

Originally from Vancouver, Canada, Mikal now lives in Oklahoma with her husband, Mark, two of their three children, and one ferocious feline who can be found napping on her desk beside her as she works each day.

You can find Mikal on Facebook, Instagram, Pinterest, Goodreads, and yes...even Twitter. ☺

# Other Books by Mikal Dawn

Emerald City Romance series
*Count Me In*
*If She Dares*
*Claim My Heart*
(also part of the Once Upon a Christmas Collection)

*A Holly, Bolly Christmas*
(part of the Something Borrowed Collection)